HOW TO
Lose A Lass

Other Books by Anna Durand

The Notorious Dr. MacT (A Hot Scots Prequel)
The British Bastard (A Hot Scots Prequel)
Dangerous in a Kilt (Hot Scots, Book One)
Wicked in a Kilt (Hot Scots, Book Two)
Scandalous in a Kilt (Hot Scots, Book Three)
The MacTaggart Brothers Trilogy (Hot Scots, Books 1-3)
Gift-Wrapped in a Kilt (Hot Scots, Book Four)
Notorious in a Kilt (Hot Scots, Book Five)
Insatiable in a Kilt (Hot Scots, Book Six)
Lethal in a Kilt (Hot Scots, Book Seven)
Irresistible in a Kilt (Hot Scots, Book Eight)
Devastating in a Kilt (Hot Scots, Book Nine)
Spellbound in a Kilt (Hot Scots, Book Ten)
Relentless in a Kilt (Hot Scots, Book Eleven)
Incendiary in a Kilt (Hot Scots, Book Twelve)
Wild in a Kilt (Hot Scots, Book Thirteen)
Unstoppable in a Kilt (Hot Scots, Book Fourteen)
Lachlan in a Kilt (The Ballachulish Trilogy, Book One)
Aidan in a Kilt (The Ballachulish Trilogy, Book Two)
Rory in a Kilt (The Ballachulish Trilogy, Book Three)
Brit vs. Scot (A Hot Brits/Hot Scots/Au Naturel Crossover Book)
The American Wives Club (A Hot Brits/Hot Scots/Au Naturel Crossover Book)
A Novel Secret (A Hot Brits/Hot Scots/Au Naturel Crossover Book)
One Hot Chance (Hot Brits, Book One)
One Hot Roomie (Hot Brits, Book Two)
One Hot Crush (Hot Brits, Book Three)
The Dixon Brothers Trilogy (Hot Brits, Books 1-3)
One Hot Escape (Hot Brits, Book Four)
One Hot Rumor (Hot Brits, Book Five)
One Hot Christmas (Hot Brits, Book Six)
One Hot Scandal (Hot Brits, Book Seven)
One Hot Deal (Hot Brits, Book Eight)
One Hot Favor (Hot Brits, Book Nine)
One Hot Bash (Hot Brits, Book Ten)
Natural Obsession (Au Naturel Nights, Book One)
Natural Deception (Au Naturel Nights, Book Two)
Natural Passion (Au Naturel Trilogy, Book One)
Natural Impulse (Au Naturel Trilogy, Book Two)
Natural Satisfaction (Au Naturel Trilogy, Book Three)
Fired Up (standalone romance)
Echo Power (Echo Power Trilogy, Book One)
Echo Dominion (Echo Power Trilogy, Book Two)
Echo Unbound (Echo Power Trilogy, Book Three)
The Janusite Trilogy (Undercover Elementals, Books 1-3)
Obsidian Hunger (Undercover Elementals, Book Four)
Unbidden Hunger (Undercover Elementals, Book Five)
The Thirteenth Fae (Undercover Elementals, Book Six)

HOW TO Lose A Lass

A Hot Scots Prequel

ANNA DURAND

JACOBSVILLE BOOKS · MARIETTA, OHIO

HOW TO LOSE A LASS

ISBN: 979-8-9852412-3-5 (paperback)
ISBN: 979-8-9852412-4-2 (ebook)
ISBN: 979-8-9852412-5-9 (audiobook)

Manufactured in the United States.

Jacobsville Books
www.JacobsvilleBooks.com

Publisher's Cataloging-in-Publication Data
provided by Five Rainbows Cataloging Services

Names: Durand, Anna, author.
Title: How to lose a lass : a hot Scots prequel / Anna Durand.
Description: Marietta, OH : Jacobsville Books, 2023. | Series: Hot Scots.
Identifiers: ISBN 978-1-958144-32-9 (paperback) | ISBN 978-1-958144-33-6 (ebook) | ISBN 978-1-958144-34-3 (audiobook)
Subjects: LCSH: Highlands (Scotland)--Fiction. | Man-woman relationships--Fiction. | Scots--Fiction. | Americans--Fiction. | Marines--Fiction. | BISAC: FICTION / Romance / Contemporary. | FICTION / Romance / Romantic Comedy. | GSAFD: Love stories.
Classification: LCC PS3604.U724 H69 2023 (print) | LCC PS3604.U724 (ebook) | DDC 813/.6--dc23.

Chapter One

Gavin

The line rings through my headset eight times before someone picks up the call. I immediately start talking. "Good afternoon, this is Gavin from Rapid React Emergency Restoration Services, the premier service provider in Minnesota. If you have a moment, I'd love to talk to you about what we can offer. If you've ever experienced an overflowing septic system or a leaking gas line, we're here to help. Whatever you need to get you back on track, we have all the options. Rapid React offers twenty-four seven, on-call packages to get you back to normal. Why don't I send you a brochure about our—"

"No, thank you," the woman on the other end of the call says curtly. "I don't need or want your services. Don't ever call me again."

She hangs up. And naturally, she slams the phone down.

I don't blame her. Cold calling must be one of the sins mentioned in the Ten Commandments, but God wrote it in invisible ink by accident. I can't believe this is what I do for a living—harass decent people. Maybe the services this company sells are useful, but the way we attract new clients just sucks. In the Marines, at least I felt like I had a purpose and a calling. Now, I'm nothing but an annoying telemarketer.

"Having a bad day, Gav?"

I lift my head to gaze at my coworker, who had spoken those strangely cheerful words. No one should be happy while working in the ninth level of hell. "Yeah, I'm not having the best day so far."

"Can't snag any new customers?"

"Nope. Everybody hangs up on me."

"Sorry, dude. That sucks." My coworker, Phil, has risen halfway out of his chair to look at me over the top of his cubicle. "But I'm sure things will get better tomorrow or the next day."

I manage only a tight smile. "Thanks for the encouragement, Phil. You're always upbeat, and I admire that."

Phil's eyes widen. "You admire *me*? I never fought in a war zone. You are a grade-A hero, Gav."

Hero? No, I don't qualify for that title. I did my duty, nothing more, nothing less. Maybe I saw things that I never want to think about again, but that doesn't make me a hero.

Phil sits back down in his cubicle, and I can just barely see the top of his bald head.

I sink back in my chair and gaze at the photo on my desk, positioned alongside my computer screen. The picture was taken years ago, and it shows my family in the last happy moments we ever had. My baby sister, Calli, grins at the camera. My parents have their arms around each other as they smile. And I stand there beside Calli, smiling just like they do.

Our happy family. It's all gone now.

Since I have nothing else to do with my life, I go back to cold calling people who mostly don't want what I'm selling. I do snag a couple new customers, though. At the end of the day, I say good night to my coworkers and head back to my tiny apartment that features inspiring decor—cement block walls, a rusty metal door, and an open design that somehow manages to still feel cramped. It would make a mole feel right at home.

After eating a so-so frozen dinner, I flop onto my worn recliner and reach for the phone, intending to call my sister, but I change my mind. It's an hour later in Michigan. She might be asleep already. Right, Calli goes to bed at seven o'clock in the evening. Duh, of course not.

I'm just about to fall asleep in my recliner when the phone rings again. I crack one eye open to see the caller ID. Then I snatch up the receiver. "Calli? Is everything okay?"

"Yeah, of course. Why do you sound panicked?"

"Uh… I don't know."

She snorts, clearly trying not to laugh at me. "That's the lamest response ever."

"Cut me some slack, C. I had a crappy day at the office, also known as the ninth level of hell."

"If you hate your job, look for something different."

I groan. "Considering how much trouble you've had finding another librarian job, you ought to know better than to tell me to just up and find something different."

"Yeah, I know. Sorry, Gav. I just want you to be happy. That's an order."

"Yes, ma'am. You can't see it, but I'm saluting."

"Ha-ha." Calli hesitates, then her tone turns sneaky. "You know, if you came to Tara's wedding, you might meet someone."

I throw my head back and groan again. "I don't want to troll for dates at our cousin's wedding. Besides, you hate it when I say things like that to you."

"Fine, I give up. Hide out in your little apartment and be miserable."

Tara had invited me to the wedding too, but my boss is sending me to Florida this weekend for a conference about how to respond to and help customers recover from home emergencies. I'd love to watch my sweet little cousin tie the knot for the second time. Blake is a good guy, unlike Tara's first husband. At least Calli hasn't married a louse like me and Tara had both done, accidentally. We're bad role models for marriage, and maybe that's why Calli has been hesitant to date, much less get into a serious relationship.

I yawn loudly.

"Fine, Gav, I get the point," Calli says with a laugh. "Go to bed. And have fun at that conference."

"Oh, yeah. Seminars about septic system restoration are always a hoot."

"Maybe you should have a one-night stand, just to get some action."

I swing the phone away from me, staring at it like the thing sprouted a set of devil horns. Yeah, I'm kind of obsessed with hell references today. "Calli Bethany Douglas, what in the world has gotten into you? My sweet baby sister would never suggest I should have a fling with a stranger."

"Sorry. I'm just worried about you."

"And I'm worried about *you*, C."

My sister sighs. "Quite a pair, aren't we?"

"Yep. Mom and Dad must be rolling over in their graves." I rub my eyes and yawn. "Better get some sleep, Calli. You've got the big wedding tomorrow."

"Good night, Gavin."

We hang up, and I drag my body over to the bed, collapsing onto it without bothering to pull the covers back or undress. Okay, I might be slightly depressed. I'll get over it. If I could recover from the shock of our parents dying in a car accident, then I can shake off this malaise too.

The next day, I fly to Florida. My sister is in Chicago this week, for Tara's wedding, but she finds time to call me and pester me about "getting back out there" so I can find my "soul mate." I tell her, "I'll do it when you do." She laughs, and that's how I know she'll be fine. Maybe Calli really will meet a guy at the wedding. Tara and Blake know lots of people, so it isn't out of the realm of possibility. Our cousin would love to find a boyfriend for Calli.

And I want both of them to be happy. They're all the family I've got.

In the evening, I enjoy dinner alone in my little hotel room. Then I try to call my sister, but she doesn't answer. Probably still hung over from the wedding reception. Nah, Calli doesn't like to drink. Maybe she spent the night with some guy. That thought does not make me feel any better. I wanted her to date, not sleep around.

After watching a bad movie on TV, I try again to get hold of Calli, but her phone goes straight to voice mail. So, I give in and leave a message. "Hey, Calli, it's me. How was the wedding bash? Tara texted me some pictures from the big event, so I know she looked gorgeous in her wedding dress. But she didn't send any pictures of you. Send some, hey? Then I'll feel like I kind of was there after all. Talk to ya later, C."

On the last day of the conference, I skip all the events and take a walk along the beach instead. The warmth of the sun feels good on my face, and I tip my head back to enjoy it. Maybe life isn't so bad after all. Three hot girls stroll past me, all wearing tiny string bikinis. They give me appreciative looks.

Yeah, I've still got it.

A few minutes later, those ladies invite me to join them at the bonfire they and their male friends had set up on the beach. They turn out to be a bunch of really nice people, and hanging out with them reminds me how good life is. I'm lucky to have a sister I love, a cousin I love, and good friends too.

But I'm still slightly worried about my sister.

When I head home in the evening, I try again to get hold of Calli. She lives in Michigan these days, which means we don't see each other as often as we'd like. I get her voicemail. Again. Well, she might still be tired from the wedding. I'm sure she'll call sooner or later. Tara is on her honeymoon, and I don't want to bother her. But after ten days of not hearing from Calli, I know something is up. Since I won't be able to relax until I banish this bad feeling, I break my vow not to bother Tara and call her. She and Blake are on Hawaii time, which must be about five hours earlier. Yeah, she won't be mad that I'm harassing her.

I *will* find out what my sister is hiding.

"Gavin? Why are you calling? Blake and I are on the beach toasting our naked bodies in the sun."

I wince hard enough that I might've popped a few veins. "Jeez, Tara, ever hear of too much information?"

"That's what you get when you interrupt my steamy honeymoon."

"Listen, I'm seriously worried about Calli. Haven't heard from her in almost two weeks, and she doesn't answer when I call."

Tara laughs in a way that she must hope will convince me that nothing's wrong.

Instead, it pricks my intuition big time. "Tell the truth, Tara. I know you know something. So, start talking."

"Well, um…" She shifts around on whatever chair she's lying on. "I suppose it's okay to tell you, since Calli never swore me to secrecy."

"Spill your guts, Tara. Now."

"Calli is shacking up with a Scottish hottie she met in Chicago."

"What?!" Yeah, I definitely shouted that loudly enough to make the entire hotel room quake. "And you weren't going to tell me about that? What if the guy's a predator?"

"Come on, Gav. You're overreacting. Calli is too smart to fall for a creep."

I think I just growled. Literally. "Where are they?"

"Well, um…at Calli's house in Michigan."

"Good girl. Now, go enjoy the rest of your honeymoon."

My sister is shacking up with some Scottish guy she just met. I still can't believe it, even while I'm flying across the Midwest to get to Calli and…save her, I guess. I didn't take the time to formulate a battle plan. I'd love to sucker punch the dirtbag, then drag him to the nearest cliff and chuck him off it. The waters of Lake Superior are very, very cold. Even if he didn't die from the fall, maybe at least his dick would get frostbite and fall off.

How could Calli not even mention that she had a boyfriend? We used to be so close, especially after our parents died. Now, she's keeping a secret from me.

Time to surprise Calli with a visit from her big brother.

I jump on an airliner and fly straight to the Houghton County Memorial Airport in the Upper Peninsula of Michigan. Then I grab a rental car and violate the speed laws to get to Calli's house in the woods.

Finally, I step onto the porch and ring the bell.

The door swings open.

Calli's eyes go wide.

I frown at her. "Why aren't you answering your phone?"

"My phone?" She stares at me blankly like she can't remember who I am or what a phone is. Then she abruptly straightens and rolls her shoulders back, meeting my gaze directly. "I've been busy."

She probably meant to say "getting busy." Christ, I never imagined my sister would ever behave this way. Calli doesn't offer any further explanation, and she doesn't move aside to let me into the house either.

I squint at her. "Are you going to tell me, or do I have to tell you?"

"Tell you what?"

I slant toward her. "I talked to Tara."

My sister does her damnedest to seem clueless, but I've known Calli all her life. She can't snow me that easily. But she tries anyway, blinking swiftly like she's confused. "What did Tara say?"

I can't help it. My fury boils up, and I flatten my lips right before I hiss, "You're living with some foreign guy."

"I'm not living with him. His motel room was damaged by a burst pipe, and he couldn't find anywhere else to stay."

"You've got a strange man in your house, not a stray puppy."

Though she clearly doesn't want me to go inside the house, I barge in anyway. No time for civility. I'm on a mission to smack down the jackass who has seduced my sister. Calli keeps behaving strangely, like when she uses her body to block my view of the hallway—not to mention her totally fake innocent expression.

My sister's crazy-but-cute puppies barrel into the house, then swiftly race down the hall with their ears pricked and their tails wagging. I have a strong suspicion about the cause of their sudden flight.

It came from Scotland and is probably screwing my sister.

Then I know for sure. How? Because a shirtless guy with wet hair, who wears only a pair of low-slung jeans, just sauntered out of the hallway.

I clench my fists so hard that my nails dig into my palms. My eyes narrow to slits, and I think my nostrils actually flare like a bull about to charge a matador.

"Hello," the Scottish asshole says in a cheerful tone. He has the gall to grin at me too.

I grit my teeth and fold my arms over my chest. "Who the hell are you?"

"Aidan MacTaggart." The bastard holds his hand out like he expects me to shake it. "And you are?"

I glare at him and curl my lip just enough to convey my feelings about this guy. "I'm the Marine who's about to kick your ass from here to Mexico."

Aidan MacTaggart seems completely unfazed by my threat. That makes me grudgingly respect him a little bit.

"Should I leave?" the guy who seduced my sister asks while running a hand through his hair. "Seems like the two of you have things to discuss."

Calli glances at him over her shoulder. "You don't have to leave. This is my brother Gavin."

Aidan smiles again, his curious gaze aimed at me. "Your brother? That does explain it."

I squint at him. "Explain what?"

"Why you're concerned about her welfare. I have three sisters, and I wouldn't like to find a man I'd never met staying in any of their homes. Especially not my younger sister."

I freeze, experiencing a sudden epiphany. One side of my mouth kinks upward. "Maybe I should go move in with your little sister."

"You could try, but Jamie lives with my older brother Rory at the moment. He's not as friendly as I am."

For some very annoying reason, hearing about the asshat's family makes me feel less...homicidal about Aidan MacTaggart. I grasp the back of my neck and frown. "I still don't like this, but...Calli's an adult. She can do what she wants."

But oh, yeah, the Scot is going down.

Chapter Two

Jamie

"Och, Rory, you and Lachlan are treating me like I'm a wee bairn." I set my hands on my hips and lift my chin just enough to get the point across to my overbearing older brothers. "I am twenty-six years old, which means I'm an adult. So please, dinnae act like I can't handle myself."

Lachlan straps his arms over his chest. "You might be twenty-six, but I am forty-two. That means you should respect my authority."

"You are not in charge of me. If I want to go to America like Aidan did, I will do it—with or without your permission."

"But Jamie—"

I hold up a hand. "Please, Lachlan, show me a wee bit of respect. I'm not a moron, and I have never done anything rash. I worked full-time at the Loch Fairbairn Library for five years, before I was made redundant, so dinnae make it sound like I'm an impulsive teenager."

Aye, I'd loved working at the library. But they simply couldn't afford to keep me on anymore.

Rory glances at Lachlan. "She's right. And if she goes to America, Aidan will make certain she doesn't get into any trouble, accidentally."

Aidan is only two years older than I am, but I understand why Lachlan and Rory believe I need my youngest brother to watch over me. In a family of six children, the eldest ones feel a responsibility to care for the rest of us. Lachlan especially feels that burden.

And maybe I am being rather pigheaded about this, but I've never left Scotland, not even to visit England. It's time I saw another part of the world.

Lachlan and Rory exchange glances, though I can't figure out what those looks mean. Until Lachie says, "I'd be more inclined to trust your judgment if you hadn't sent that text message to Aidan."

Oh, aye, he had to bring that up. When Aidan had gone to Chicago to find an American wife, no one tried to stop him. I might have sent Aidan a cheeky text shortly after his arrival in America, but only because MacTaggarts love to harass each other. I had asked him, "Have you found your quarry, Don Juan? Expect details about American fling." That's nothing compared to what Lachlan did when he was in Chicago.

I cannae let him get away with implying that I'm the irresponsible one. "The man who had a four-week fling with an American woman and then ripped her heart to shreds has no grounds for chastising me for teasing Aidan."

Lachlan winces. "Aye, ye have a point."

Rory shakes his head at Lachie. "You caved without a fight. It's a sad state of affairs when a Scotsman lets his wee sister cow him. She's right, though. You treated Erica badly, yet she married you anyway. I will never marry again, so none of my siblings will have any fodder to use against me."

That sounds like a vow destined to be broken. I know Rory has terrible luck with women, and his three ex-wives clearly did more damage to his psyche than any of us know. But I believe with all my heart that he will find the right lass eventually. I want him to be happy.

Now that the family conference about how poor wee Jamie needs her brothers to run her life is over, I go for a walk to clear my head. My brothers can't stop me if I want to fly to America to visit Aidan and possibly meet a man. I've saved up enough money to pay for an airline ticket—economy class, of course. I don't relish a long flight in a cramped seat, but I'll do whatever it takes. I need to see more of the world than just Loch Fairbairn and my hometown of Ballachulish.

On my stroll down the streets of Loch Fairbairn, I bump into a few people I know. We say hello and smile at each other. Aye, I do love my home. But that doesn't change the fact that I need to expand my horizons. An entire world full of new places and new people awaits me out there.

I've just passed by my cousin Kirsty's metaphysical shop, which isn't open right now. It's after five o'clock. I would've liked to get her opinion on my plans to visit America, but that will have to wait. Kirsty went to university in England, so she might be able to help me convince my brothers to let me go on holiday alone.

The following day, Lachlan and Rory try one more time to talk me out of going to America. I understand their concerns, and I even appreciate that they want to look out for me. But I am a grown woman. And my one serious relationship crashed and burned, leaving me confused and saddened by the loss of someone I had thought I would spend the rest of my life with. Trevor wasn't the right one after all. So, I will go elsewhere to hunt—um, *look* for a different sort of man. No, I shouldn't use the word hunt if I mean to get my brothers on my side in this matter. That sounds like I'll be scouring seedy clubs for a "hook-up," as my new sister-in-law Erica would say. I'm looking for a good man, not a one-night lover.

Thinking about Erica spurs me to pay her a visit. I arrive at the farmhouse to find Lachlan putting up fencing for the chickens I can see waddling about in a temporary fenced enclosure.

He waves to me and calls out, "*Madainn mhath*, Jamie. We weren't expecting to see you today."

"I came to see Erica."

He sets down the implements he'd been using and saunters over to me, where I've just stepped out of my car. "You want my wife? If you're planning to get her on your side with the barmy American man-hunt idea—"

"Och, Lachie, ye make it sound like I mean to brainwash her. Erica is very clever, and I need some advice from a woman."

"Dinnae expect Erica to condone your plan, just because of, ah…" Lachie winces and scratches his cheek. "How we met."

I roll my eyes. "Honestly, everyone knows the story of how you met Erica when you were trolling underground clubs for an anonymous shag. But that's not what I want her advice about."

Lachlan twists his mouth into a disapproving expression. But then he sighs, and his shoulders flag. "All right, go on."

Though I didn't need or want his permission, I decide not to harass him anymore. When I walk into the house, I find Erica in the kitchen with their wee bairn, my nephew Nicholas.

She notices me and smiles. "Hi, Jamie. What can I do for you?"

"I was hoping for a bit of advice. I'm sure Lachlan told you about my plan."

"Yep. My husband isn't too happy about that, but I told him he needs to stop treating you like a child just because you're the youngest sibling."

For a couple of seconds, I can't speak. "You don't think I'm insane?"

She laughs softly. "No, sweetie, I don't. You are a very smart cookie, and besides, you'll be with Aidan when you go to America. Probably won't meet a lot of single men in the wilds of Michigan, but who knows. I never thought I'd meet the love of my life in an underground club in Chicago."

"Thank you, Erica. Can I help you with your cooking?"

"Why don't you hang out with Nicky in the living room while I whip up lunch?"

"Aye, I'd love to spend time with my nephew."

My lunch with Erica and Lachlan is lovely, but I never imagined it would result in me getting what I wanted. But that very evening, that's what happens. I've been staying with Rory in his castle, Dùndubhan, for a while now. This evening, Rory and I are in the sitting room enjoying hot cocoa. All right, I'm drinking cocoa. Rory prefers to sip whisky.

Then Lachlan bursts into the room. "Did ye tell her yet, Rory?"

My most taciturn brother turns his head to look at Lachlan. "I thought I was meant to wait for you."

"Well, I'm here now. So, tell the lass."

Rory faces me. "Lachlan, Aidan, and I had a teleconference earlier and reached a decision. You may go to America, but you will travel on my jet."

"*Our* jet," Lachlan corrects. "We share it. Or have ye conveniently forgotten that?"

"Aye, fine, *our* jet."

Did my brothers actually just agree to let me go to America? I think they did. "When can I leave?"

My brothers glance at each other again, and Lachlan sighs heavily. "Tomorrow morning."

"I'd rather leave tonight. Maybe my Prince Charming is waiting for me in America."

Rory's expression becomes rather grave. "I wish you weren't so dead-set on finding a man. It's bad enough that Aidan is living with a woman he just met, but I worry more for you than I do for him. With good reason."

"I know that, Rory. But you know I'm not an eejit. Besides, Aidan will pick me up at the airport and keep an eye on me for you."

"Then you've given up on the idea of staying at Erica's house in Chicago."

"No. But I can visit with Aidan and his lass, then go to Chicago for a weekend."

Lachlan rubs his jaw. "We've done all we can do, Rory. Jamie won't give up, and the best we can do is make sure she's in safe hands. Aidan's lass has offered to let Jamie stay with them at her house in Michigan. We all know Aidan won't let anything happen to Jamie. But you will wait until tomorrow."

I can't wait to fall in love. I've dreamed about my Prince Charming since I was a little girl, and that desire has become even stronger lately. The men I've dated left me feeling less than enthusiastic about my prospects for getting married and starting a family, but I can't give up yet. I need to do something drastic to change my life and achieve my goals.

And my brothers have finally agreed to help me do that.

I rush up to Lachlan and kiss his cheek, then do the same for Rory. Cannae help grinning. "Thank you so much. I love you both."

"We love you too, Jamie. And if some American *cacan* breaks your heart, we will hunt him down and batter him."

The evening after my brothers gave up on changing my mind, I stand on the tarmac at the Inverness airport surrounded by my family, while they hug me and haver about how much they'll miss me. My sisters, Catriona and Fiona, urge me to be careful but also wish me success in finding an American man. The fact that Lachlan married an American lass proved to be the final nail in the coffin of the idea that I shouldn't leave home for a holiday on another continent.

"Scottish men can be so bloody pigheaded," Fiona says. "Maybe we should all try Americans instead."

I nod with sarcastic gravity. "Oh, aye, Catriona should definitely try that. Her British Bastard broke her heart, so she might as well branch out into another country."

Our father overheard what I said and saunters over to us. "What's wrong with a good Scotsman? Plenty of those for you lasses to choose from."

Ma hooks her arm around Da's and gives him a patient smile. "Let Jamie make her own decisions, Niall. Besides, after testing out American men, she might well decide to marry a Scot after all."

"As long as she's happy, that's all that matters."

Lachlan walks up the stairs with me, keeping a light hold on my elbow as we climb to the open door of the private jet. He walks with me onto the plane too. Then he hugs me. "Be careful, *gràidh*. You've never left Scotland before, and America is much different from our home here in the Highlands. Aidan will take care of you, but…" He hugs me again and kisses the top of my head. "You are my baby sister. I will always worry about you."

"If I find the right man, you won't need to worry so much." I make a shooing motion. "Now go on, Lachie. I don't think Erica wants you to escort me all the way to Michigan."

"No, my wife wouldn't like that."

My brother shuffles over to the door, then pauses to glance back at me. He smiles a little, seeming a wee bit melancholy.

I smile and wave. He'll get over his worry once he knows I'm with Aidan.

Lachlan finally exits the jet, and a moment later, one of the pilots emerges from the cockpit to close the door.

I rush over to a sofa that lies up against the wall and kneel on the seat to watch out the windows as the plane begins to roll down the runway. My throat tightens. My eyes burn. I'm about to cry, but that's rubbish. A grown woman doesn't cry simply because she's leaving her home for the first time. I never went away to university in England like my siblings did, instead choosing to earn my degree close to home. I certainly haven't visited America before, though Cat had done that when she was a grad student.

Once the initial rush of excitement wears off, I realize just how dead boring a long flight to another country really is. Traveling alone is, well, rather lonely. The pilots take turns visiting with me, apparently because they feel sorry for the lassie who's traveling alone. I appreciate the effort, but it only makes me feel more isolated. I've always been surrounded by MacTaggarts, from my brothers and sisters to my many cousins.

After three hours, I need to talk to someone I know. But instead of ringing either of my sisters, I dial the number for my cousin Jack. He groans when he picks up the call, sounding as if he'd been asleep.

"Hello, Jack, it's Jamie."

"Who?" He yawns loudly. "Bloody hell, Jamie. It's after midnight."

"Sorry. I just wondered if—Oh, never mind."

"You rang me, so now you need to explain yourself. Are ye already feeling homesick? I heard you were off on an American adventure."

Leave it to a psychotherapist to realize that without me saying a word. "Aye, I'm a wee bit homesick. I've tried to sleep, but I feel restless."

"Of course you do, *gràidh*. You're excited and anxious at the same time, which is to be expected when you're away on a holiday in another country—on another continent."

"You always know how to make me feel better, Jack. You're a wonderful therapist."

He chuckles. "I appreciate the compliment. But I haven't done anything. You just needed a sounding board, and I was glad to serve that purpose for you. Now, let's both go to bed. Aye?"

"You're right. Good night, Jack."

"Good night, Jamie. And have fun in America—if Aidan will let you. I doubt he's pleased with your plan to find an American man to marry."

"Why would Aidan care? He's Don Juan MacTaggart, after all. I expect he'll be happy about my plan. Aidan did fly to America to find a lass for himself."

Jack chuckles again. "Och, Jamie, you don't understand brothers. Good night again, lass."

By the time I wake in the wee hours of the morning, we're already flying across Michigan on our way to the Upper Peninsula. I eat a quick breakfast, then gaze out the windows, too excited to simply relax on the sofa or read a magazine. The closer we come to the Houghton County Memorial Airport, the more excited I feel. My pulse has quickened. As the jet descends, I move onto a window seat and stare out at the landscape that reveals itself little by little. I see trees, but at first, I can't make out much detail. Then it all comes into view. I have never seen a forest as lush and gorgeous as the ones here in the Upper Peninsula of Michigan. I watch the waters of Lake Superior as they whisk by beneath the jet and see whitewater splashing and breakers crashing onto the shore. We fly over what looks like a lift bridge too.

My American adventure is about to begin.

Chapter Three

Gavin

This morning, I feel surprisingly good. Maybe I don't like that my sister is shacking up with a virtual stranger, but that's one damn good reason why I need to stick around until I either figure out that Aidan isn't a scam artist or I've beaten him to death with a tree branch and buried the body in the woods where no one will ever find it. Yeah, it's possible I'm overreacting. But Calli is my family. She's my baby sister, and without our parents around to watch out for her, I'm the only one who can protect her.

While I lie here in the hunting shack, with only a comforter as a mattress, I reminisce about yesterday. I'd returned to the house after stashing my stuff in the shack, and I'd walked in on Aidan smooching with my sister. When I cleared my throat deliberately, Calli scuttled away from the Scottish guy. But Aidan simply gazed at me steadily, as if he had no intention of explaining himself or apologizing for making out with my sister in my presence.

Not that doing it in private would make me happy either.

During dinner, I'd razzed Aidan some more, strictly to find out what his limits are. He doesn't seem to have a button I can push to make him fly off the handle. Okay, that's good to know. He also doesn't seem to give a damn what I think, though he clearly wants to reassure me that Calli is in safe hands with him. He didn't say that outright, but I could tell that was what he meant every time he talked about his family.

The guy has five siblings. *Five.* The MacTaggarts have an even lineup, with three brothers and three sisters. Today, I'll meet one of his relatives—his sister Jamie.

As I'd exited the house last night, I'd called out over my shoulder, "I'll be within earshot of the house, Romeo."

"I'm known as Don Juan MacTaggart, not Romeo."

"Whatever." I raised two fingers and aimed them at him, then at my own eyes. "I'll be watching you, MacTaggart."

Aidan had smiled with no small amount of sarcasm. "That's very comforting. I'll sleep better just knowing you're there."

While he was in the master bedroom screwing my sister.

I get dressed and head for the house, ready for another round of former Marine versus cocky Scot. But I know that this morning, Calli and Aidan will be heading for the airport to pick up his little sister. They had invited me to go with them, but that seemed kind of weird. I don't know Jamie. She might feel uncomfortable with a stranger standing there beside her brother.

How old is Jamie MacTaggart? I hadn't thought to ask yesterday. She's probably a cute little fifteen-year-old who has pigtails and wears a plaid skirt. Aidan's older brother, Rory, had let his sister fly to America on his private jet all alone. So maybe she's a little older than fifteen. I'll find out soon enough.

Now, I climb down from the little shack, which has a wooden ladder for accessing the interior. Then I jog the short distance to the house and try to open the sliding glass doors at the back side. It won't budge. Calli must have locked the doors overnight. I knock on the glass.

Calli emerges from the hallway dressed in a satin robe. She halts and peers at me from across the living room.

I'm standing here with one hand in my jeans pockets and the other knocking on the glass, waiting to be admitted into the house. The puppies race up to me from behind. I'd come through the yard gate and hadn't noticed Mandy and Misty. They must've been around the corner of the house, where there's a small area that's part of the yard. Now, they jump up and down while licking my hands and pawing at my jeans. Jeez, women were never this excited to see me. Calli's puppies have always been kind of hyper.

I wave at Calli.

Finally, my sister secures her robe more tightly around herself and trots over here to open the doors.

Misty starts bouncing up and down like a pogo stick, her feet lifting several inches off the ground with every bounce. The puppy manages to slather her tongue over my hand while still pogo-sticking around me.

I grimace. Slimy puppy saliva isn't my favorite thing. Who knows what these dogs have eaten today? Might be rotting rat carcasses or smelly insects.

Calli aims an overly cheerful smile at me. She's trying too hard for sure. "Morning, Gav. Are the girls being pests?"

"No, they're fine." The only pest in the vicinity is the asshat who seduced my sister. "You planning to let me in? Or is what's-his-name walking around buck naked in there?"

"Of course you can come in, Gavin."

She moves aside, waving for me to walk into the house.

I shuffle inside and throw Calli a sidelong glance.

My sister bites her lip and hunches her shoulders.

The puppies bound after me while I make a beeline for the kitchen bar and mutter, "So glad Mom and Dad aren't here to see this. Calli shacking up with a stranger."

Calli clearly didn't hear what I said, and I never intended for her to hear it. As much as I don't like this situation, I have no choice but to accept it for now. So, I let out an annoyed sigh and park my ass on the nearest stool, facing my sister.

Mandy and Misty had followed me into the house, and now, their ears perk up like they heard something. Their heads swivel toward the hallway in unison. Then the puppies take off in the direction of the spare bedroom.

They must have heard or smelled the Scottish asshat. I hope he slept alone last night, but I kind of doubt it. Something way more disturbing has happened, though, and I forget all about Don Juan. Surprise makes me stop blinking briefly, and I point at Calli's face. "You're blushing."

She lays a hand on her cheek, seeming as surprised as I am.

"Why are you blushing, Calli?" I wait for five seconds—yeah, I counted—and then rest one arm on the bar and drum my fingers on the surface. "You're sleeping with him, aren't you?"

My sister marches up to me and lifts her chin while trying to give me a tough stare. "Do you really want to talk about my sex life?"

Oh, shit. I should've thought about that before I asked if she was screwing Aidan. Because no, I do not want to hear about Calli's sex life. The very idea of that makes me a little queasy. "No, I don't need to hear about that."

"Then accept that it's none of your business."

I frown and tap one finger on the countertop. "What's wrong with you, C? For years, you didn't even date—as far as I know. When I called a week ago, you didn't say anything about a guy, and now you're shacked up with him. I don't understand, that's all."

Calli just stares at me.

The look of despair on her face shatters me, and I soften my tone. "I'm sorry, okay? Maybe it is none of my business. But I love you, Calli. You're the only family I've got—besides Tara, who's a good kid but kind of ditsy. You're supposed to be my level-headed sister, the one I can count on to make sense."

"Sorry I disappointed you. But you're acting like I committed a capital offense by getting involved with a man. I like Aidan. You've been spending time with him. Do you really think he's a Euro-trash gigolo taking advantage of me?"

I slump on the stool and release a long sigh. "No. I don't think that."

Barking erupts from down the hallway, a sure sign that Don Juan is about to waltz into the living room. Calli's expression shifts from anxious to excited in a heartbeat.

I gape at her. "Now you're smiling. I may not like you sleeping with Aidan, but I have to admit I've never seen you this happy before. Ever. When you look at him, you get…gushy."

Calli stares at me, eyes wide.

I nod slowly. "Yep, that's right. You moon over him, and I'm guessing you don't even realize you're doing it. Man, you've got it bad, don't you?"

She clamps her teeth down on her lips and veers her gaze to the kitchen cabinets.

Oh, yeah, I know exactly what's going on here. I can't help laughing a little bit, though it's not derisive. "At least promise me if you marry him, you won't move to Scotland."

Her gaze veers back to me. "I'm not marrying Aidan."

"No? You say that like there's no way in hell you'd even consider it. You always wanted to get married. I remember you acting out fake weddings between your Barbie and Ken dolls."

"That was a long time ago."

I tip my head to the side, studying her. "What happened to you, C? Whatever's going on with you, I hope you know you can tell me about it."

Her mouth opens, like she's about to speak.

But then Don Juan himself saunters into the living room, and any chance I had to get the truth out of Calli has vanished. For now, at least.

After breakfast, Calli and Aidan jump in the fancy car his brother had rented for him and head for the airport. The puppies and I watch bad talk shows on TV while we wait for the new guest to arrive. Eventually, I give up on the talk shows and return to my little cabin for a while, if only to get a brief break from the sweet but extremely rambunctious puppies.

I've just started to make my way back to the house when I hear the distinctive sound of gravel crunching on the driveway. Calli and the Scots must be pulling up. The puppies race into the house, making the dog door thwap, just as I reach the sliding glass doors. I push them open, stepping inside. Calli and Aidan stand near the front door, holding hands. But I can't focus on that for long enough to say something snarky. No, my full attention is consumed by the beautiful girl who giggles as Mandy and Misty lick her shapely ankles.

Who is that?

Her long, golden-brown hair shivers every time she moves her head, and her hazel eyes shimmer with flecks of emerald green. Damn, she's gorgeous. When she smiles, I swear I can feel the warmth of that expression infiltrating me.

"You can love me more later," the girl tells the puppies. Then she straightens, smoothing out her skirt, and turns toward me. "You must be Calli's brother. I'm Jamie, Aidan's sister."

I swallow hard and suddenly can't remember how to speak, not coherently, anyway. I might be speaking gibberish, but I can't focus on any of the words that come out of my mouth. "Hey. Nice to, uh, meet you. I'm Gavin. Douglas. Calli's brother, Gavin Douglas."

Jamie smiles at me, and the cutest dimples form in her cheeks. "Nice to meet you too, Gavin."

She must think I'm a complete moron. Jamie MacTaggart is not a pigtailed girl but a full-grown and voluptuous woman. I can't seem to get my brain in gear while I'm looking at her, which is something I've never experienced before. I've never seen a woman as beautiful and sweet as Aidan's little sister.

I suddenly realize I'm holding Jamie's hand. Did we shake hands? I've got no frigging idea. But her palm feels warm and soft, and that fact makes me wonder how warm and soft she is everywhere else. I swear she's gazing at me with the same desire that I've felt since the moment I laid eyes on her.

Aidan grasps Jamie's wrist and tugs, but she doesn't release my hand. His lips pucker, and he tugs again. "Let me show you to your room."

Yeah, he spoke those words in a tone that proves he's not as unflappable as he likes for me to think. Aidan is getting irritated. Well, now he knows how I felt when I found him shacking up with my baby sister.

But I still can't tear my focus away from Jamie.

Aidan drags Jamie away from me, forcing us to let go of each other's hands as he hauls her down the hallway. She keeps glancing back at me and smiling. Once the two of them disappear from view, Calli rounds on me.

She plants her hands on her hips, and her lips kink up on one side in a sly, smug smile. "Gee, Gav, looks to me like you're going gushy over Aidan's sister."

"What?" I blink several times quickly, but that only breaks about eighty percent of my trance. "I was being friendly to your guest, that's all."

"Uh-huh. Flirting is a requirement for proper etiquette?"

I splutter because I still can't think straight, and Calli's being ridiculous. "All I said was hello."

My sister grins. "No, you said 'uh, hey, nice to meet you, can I please shave your legs for you.' Right before you mooned at her."

"I did not say that."

"Okay, maybe I ad-libbed the shaving part. But you were stammering and gaping at her like you'd never seen a pretty girl before."

I clench my teeth. "I'm not the one getting naked with somebody I barely know."

"But you'd like to make time with Aidan's little sister."

"Well—" Damn, she's right. And I hate that. Maybe I don't like the Aidan-Calli situation, but I've pretty much lost all my leverage in that regard since the moment I saw Jamie. I shove my hands into my jeans pockets. "You're a grown-up, so you can do what you want."

Calli struggles not to grin at me again. "Gee, thanks, Gav."

No matter what Calli says, I never "mooned" at Jamie MacTaggart.

I might've gawked. A little. Hardly at all, really.

Jeez, I am so screwed.

Chapter Four

Jamie

od an Donais, Gavin Douglas is the handsomest and sexiest man I've ever seen. No film star could compete with his looks, his muscular body, or his voice. I could listen to him read the phone book, followed by a recitation of the Encyclopedia Britannica. Oh, aye, everything about Gavin turns me on. If Aidan likes Calli, then her brother must be a good person too. He's spent a day or two with Gavin and Calli, so he must have gotten to know the man with the beautiful, pale-brown eyes.

A sigh rushes out of me. I could gaze into Gavin's eyes all day long.

My brother virtually drags me into what looks like a guest bedroom. I got a glimpse of another, larger bedroom at the end of the hall, which must be the main suite. That means Calli sleeps in there. That realization brings up questions I need to ask my brother.

Aidan shuts the door behind us and frowns at me.

I set my hands on my hips. "Are you sleeping with Calli?"

"None of your business, Jamie."

"Ooh, Aidan the Magnificent is getting testy. This must be a first. After all, you're the cheerful one who never growls at anybody." I can't help smirking. "But you've fallen head over heels for Calli Douglas, and ye dinnae want to talk about that, do you?"

"Ahmno head over heels." He thumps the top of his head with one fist. "See? My head is still on top."

"Very funny. But I can't give up on harassing you. Might as well answer my question, or else you'll have no leverage to make me tell you anything."

My brother flattens his lips and squints at me for a moment. Then he bows his head and blows out a breath. "*Mhac na galla*. You're right, but I still can't answer your question. It wouldn't be chivalrous to share that information."

"All right, I understand that. I'm sorry for poking my nose into your business, but you were being a bit overbearing."

"I'm sorry for that."

"Thank you." I tip my head to the side and study him. "You really like this lass, don't you? The man who loves women finally found one who makes him want more than a fling."

"Aye, I do feel that way about Calli."

I sit down on the bed, clasping my hands on my lap. "You said you'd find an American wife, and you did."

He sits down beside me. "Calli isn't my wife, not yet. And I dinnae know if she ever will be."

"The way she looks at you, I'd say it's a dead certainty you will marry her."

"What about you and Gavin?"

I roll my eyes. "Honestly, Aidan, I met the man thirty seconds ago. I'm attracted to him, but that's all."

"Aye, of course. I'm sorry." He pushes up off the bed. "We should go back out there."

I trail after Aidan as we exit the guest bedroom. He walks rather more swiftly than seems necessary, but I reckon he's anxious about me and Gavin—or maybe he's worried about whether Calli will ever marry him.

Gavin is nowhere in sight. That fact makes me feel a wee bit deflated.

But I recover quickly and sit on the sofa with Calli. "Sooo, we should get to know each other, Calli. Since you're going to be my sister-in-law."

Aidan throws his hands up, his jaw drops, and he flaps his head. "I didn't say a word to her."

"You didn't need to, Aidan. I have eyes, and ahmno an eejit. Besides, you told everyone you were coming to America to find a wife like Lachlan did."

Aidan shifts his attention to Calli, his expression almost pleading, as if he hopes she can save him from having to discuss the subject any further.

Calli speaks to me but keeps her focus on Aidan. "It's a bit early to think about that."

I lift my brows. "Aye, but Aidan has a way of convincing women to do almost anything."

"Does he now."

Aidan's jaw drops again as he shakes his head.

Calli puckers her lips, but it seems like a teasing expression.

I decide to take pity on the pair of them and change the subject. "Where's Gavin?"

"He's staying in the hunting cabin out in the woods," Calli tells me. "We'll see him again at lunch."

I sag against the sofa. No Gavin until lunch? I want to chat to him and… I don't know. Well, if I'm completely honest with myself, I want to beg him to shag me. I've never been the sort of lass who engages in casual sex, though. Something about Gavin makes me want to do all manner of wild things.

We could shag in that hunting cabin.

Bloody hell. What is wrong with me?

Since Aidan and Calli clearly need a bit of time alone to discuss things, I take a shower in the guest bedroom. Washing off all that travel grime feels wonderful, especially since the guest bathroom includes lovely little scented soaps and soft shower poufs.

I do see Gavin at lunch, though Aidan insists that I sit beside him at the table while Gavin and Calli sit on the opposite side. Neither man wants his sister to be within touching distance of the other. Our conversations revolve around boring things like the weather, the scenery, and the tourist destinations in the area. I would love to explore the Keweenaw Peninsula, which I've just learned is the name of this part of the Upper Peninsula of Michigan. And I now know all about the copper mining that used to take place in this region, beginning in ancient times and then starting up again thousands of years later in the eighteen hundreds.

I want to chat to Gavin alone. When Calli gives me a tight smile, I'm dead sure that she wants to be alone with Aidan too.

Calli gets what she wants when Aidan takes her into the master bedroom. They both seem tired, just like I am and Gavin must be too.

Gavin simply walks out the back door and disappears into the woods, carrying a large, battery-operated torch.

While I'm lying in bed, trying to sleep, I keep fantasizing about sneaking into that wee cabin so I can crawl under the covers and lick my way down his chest, lower and lower, until I reach his cock. Those fantasies make me so randy that I need to *fannadh*, but touching myself isn't as fulfilling as shagging Gavin would be. With a body like his, he could drive me to the heights of ecstasy. No man has ever done that for me. The laddies I've dated just wanted a quick poke, then they either left or rolled over and fell asleep.

Somehow, I know Gavin wouldn't be like that.

In the evening, we're all jeeked. It's been an exhausting but wonderful day, getting to know Calli and especially Gavin. He has a wry sense of humor that I love, and every time he looks at me, I feel like he wants to kiss me. I want that, for sure. Being this attracted to a man I met this morning seems irrational, but I dinnae care.

A big yawn splits my mouth open. Time for bed, alone.

I amble down the hallway and pop my head through the open doorway to Calli and Aidan's room, wishing them a good night. Then I shuffle into my room, shut the door, and collapse onto the bed. I almost forget to change into my pajamas, but quickly realize I don't want to sleep while fully clothed. The moment I've curled up under the covers, I fall asleep.

When I wake in the morning, I feel more refreshed than I have in ages. Maybe it's the clean Michigan air doing that to me. Dinnae care what the reason is. All right, maybe I do have a clue why I feel this way. The word starts with a G and ends with "avin."

I wander out of my room, heading for the kitchen. Maybe I'll cook breakfast for Calli and Aidan, to show my appreciation for the way they've handled my attraction to Gavin. Aidan clearly wanted to tell me to go home right away, but he didn't do it. He understands that I'm a grown woman and not a bloody eejit.

Something crackles under my foot just as I've reached the bar. It's a scrap of crumpled paper that was ripped from a larger sheet, but there's nothing on it. I bend over to pick it up.

"Good morning, Jamie. Thanks for the fantastic wake-up call."

The sound of Gavin's voice makes every hair on my body stand up. A thrill rushes through me, and I spin round to smile at him. "I didn't give you a wake-up call, since I had no idea you were here."

"Oh, you woke me up for damn sure." He skims his gaze over my body, clearly noting my pajamas that consist of short-shorts and a skimpy top that has spaghetti straps. My nipples are jutting too, thanks to the way his sexy voice affects me. Gavin licks his lips, then veers his attention to my face. "That's a view any man would love to see first thing in the morning."

When I had bent over, did he get a glimpse of my cleavage? Part of me hopes he got a full view of my tits. But it isn't fair. I haven't glimpsed any naughty bits of him.

I toss the paper into the rubbish bin and wave toward the kitchen. "I was just about to make breakfast for all of us."

He eyes me up and down again. "Would you like to go for a walk first? Our keepers aren't up yet."

"A walk would be lovely."

Gavin gives me a sensual smile and winks. "Might want to get dressed first. It's mating season out there, and your PJs would draw in all the horny bucks."

"I thought deer rutted in the fall. It's still summer."

He chuckles. "I'm sure you could make every male of every species as horny as hell. You've sure done that to me."

I can't believe we're discussing the rutting habits of animals. But oddly, I am getting randy. "Wait here while I get dressed. Then we'll go for a walk."

As I'm leaving the guest room, now fully clothed and ready for a nature hike, I bump into Aidan. He's just left the room he shares with Calli, and he discreetly shuts the door behind him.

"*Madainn mhath*, Jamie." He studies me briefly. "You seem even more cheerful than usual. Gavin must be in the house, aye?"

"He is." I fold my arms over my chest. "You're very relaxed and satisfied this morning, so Calli must be in that bedroom. Aye?"

"When did you become a *smuilceag*? My sweet little sister never would have discussed my sex life."

My brother just called me a chit. I am cheeky, but only because Aidan started it. "If ye dinnae want me to comment on your love life, then don't comment on mine."

"I'm glad to see you so happy, that's all I meant."

Lifting onto my toes, I kiss his cheek. "And I'm glad to see you so happy too."

We stroll into the living room together.

Gavin is sitting on a stool at the bar. When he sees Aidan, his brows lift. "Are you coming for a walk with us?"

"No, I'll stay here. Calli is still sleeping. But you two should go out there and enjoy the wilderness."

Calli emerges from the master bedroom then, dressed and wearing a soft smile. When she sees Aidan, her expression broadens into a glowing grin. My brother slips an arm round her waist, tugging her into his side. "Now that you're awake, *gràidh*, we should all have breakfast together. Gavin and Jamie can delay their walk until later."

I glance at Gavin, who shrugs. "Aye, we can wait. I'll make breakfast."

Gavin leaps off the stool. "I'll help you."

"Thank you."

He winces. "Fair warning. I'm not the best chef in the world."

I clasp his hand. "We don't need a five-star chef. The full Scottish breakfast isn't posh."

"Good. Then I'm definitely in."

Aidan and Calli snuggle up on the sofa to watch television while Gavin and I have fun cooking up a meal for the four of us. He might not be an expert cook, but he listens to my advice and instructions, following them precisely. Soon, we have a delicious breakfast feast ready to eat. We go out into the backyard to enjoy the food at the picnic table. Calli's dogs, Mandy and Misty, stay close by to snap up any tidbits that might fall onto the grass.

After breakfast, my brother suggests we should play Monopoly. Gavin and Calli don't understand why, not until Aidan tells them that Lachlan and Erica had played the game when they first met. It's become a sort of MacTaggart family legend. Aidan adds elements to the story that Lachlan never mentioned. I'm fair certain Calli and Gavin realize my brother is concocting a porky, but they play along for the fun of it.

We play six rounds of Monopoly. I win four of them. Gavin wins one, and Calli also wins one. Aidan couldn't get out of jail.

Gavin insists on making lunch alone. That surprises me, and I have to ask a question.

"I thought you didn't know how to cook," I say. "Just this morning, you told us that you aren't skilled at crafting meals."

"And it's true. But I can whip up a mean hamburger."

He does just that too. Gavin seasoned the ground beef with "secret ingredients" that he wouldn't divulge, not even to me. I leaned over to whisper into his ear that I'd make it worth his while if he shared the secret. But he only smirked and said, "You could torture it out of me, and I wouldn't mind at all."

Oh, aye, this man has captivated me. And I love it.

Chapter Five

Gavin

idan decided to stay in the house while I take the girls out into the fenced backyard to play with the puppies. They worship Jamie and can't seem to stop themselves from licking every inch of her exposed skin. I'd love to do that too, but in a different way. For a few minutes, the three of us take turns tossing a toy around for the puppies. Then Jamie and I start to excuse ourselves so we can enjoy that walk we'd planned on taking.

But Calli has a different suggestion. "Why don't you guys take the puppies with you? They love to get out of the yard, and I have retractable leashes for them."

I roll my eyes. "They'll probably yank us off our feet, using their leashes to drag us around while we're flat on our bellies."

"You love my girls, Gavin. Why else would you roll around on the ground tickling their tummies?"

Jamie laughs. "Gavin does that?"

"Absolutely. He's a softy at heart."

I aim a sarcastically stern look at her. "Don't spread that rumor, Calli. I have a badass rep to uphold."

Jamie nudges me with her elbow. "You don't need to uphold your reputation. Everyone who sees you knows you're a powerful man."

My sister puckers her lips like she's desperately trying not to smirk.

I squint at her. "You better not be laughing at me in your mind."

Calli's laughter splutters out of her.

Sighing, I shake my head at her. "I might need to disown you, C. No way can I have a sister who's a… What did you call it, Jamie?"

"A *smuilceag*. It means she's a cheeky chit."

"Yeah, that fits Calli to a tee."

Jamie eyes me sideways. "Do you even know what a chit is?"

"Hey, I've watched British TV shows. A chit is a sassy girl."

My sister never used to be quite so sarcastic, but I have to admit, I like this new side of her. She's a stronger person than she used to be, though I can still see traces of the fear she's been hiding for years. Calli has never wanted to talk about it. I know at least part of the reason for that fear stems from that guy Rade. For now, I won't interrogate her about that. Instead, I'll spend the afternoon strolling through the woods with the prettiest girl I've ever seen and the world's most insane puppies.

Calli goes into the house. I'm positive I don't want to know what she and Aidan will be getting up to while I'm enjoying an innocent walk with Jamie. Don Juan will probably screw my sister on the sofa.

"Are we away?" Jamie asks. "That means do you want to go yet?"

"Guess that's the Scottish way of saying that. It's cute." We already have the leashes on the puppies. I hand one leash to Jamie. "You can take Mandy. She's smaller and should be easier for you to handle. Misty can be a jumping bean and could knock you over if she catches you off guard."

"I can handle two wee pups."

A laugh snorts out of me. "These dogs are fifty times stronger than they look."

"Hmm, are you afraid you can't handle three girls?"

"Three?" I suddenly realize what she meant and can't resist taking the bait. "Mandy and Misty can be rambunctious, but you will be putty in my hands."

"I'd like that."

Once we reach the gate, I swing it open to let the three ladies go first. Then I slip my hand into Jamie's palm. Her head jerks up, and her lips curl into a sweetly surprised smile—and she threads her fingers with mine. I haven't even taken her on a real date. Maybe this is the backwards way of wooing a woman, but I don't give a damn. Doing it the so-called right way ended in heartbreak. I might have just met Jamie yesterday, but I already know she would never treat me the way Leanne did.

I lead my little harem down the widest path in these woods. Most game trails are pretty narrow, but the people who used to live in the house that Calli's been renting widened those trails. They must've liked to go for walks. The old hunting cabin, which is really more of a shack, had been built by a previous owner.

We talk about silly things, like movies and music. She informs me that bagpipes are the best instrument on earth, but I know she's only trying to test my limits of how Scottish I want to go. For her, I'd change my accent and wear a kilt every day. And yeah, I tell her that.

Jamie laughs, and it's the sweetest sound I've ever heard. "You don't need to go that far. Even my brothers don't wear kilts every day." She already had her arm hooked around mine, but now she snuggles up to me and rests her chin on my arm. "I would never want you to change your accent. I love the way you talk."

"Thanks. I love the way you talk too."

"You're so sweet, Gavin. I wouldn't have expected that from a former military man."

"Have you met a lot of those types?"

"Aye. I have cousins who served, like Munro, Logan, and Magnus. My friend Thane Buchanan also served." She studies me for a moment as we continue strolling through the woods. "They fought in combat situations. Were you sent to a war zone too?"

"Yeah, in Afghanistan."

"I had a feeling you must have seen combat. The men I know who were in the military have the same sort of reticence about their pasts."

Am I reticent? Well, I guess I must be. Never considered the possibility. But talking about my past isn't my favorite thing to do.

Jamie rests her cheek on my arm. "It's all right if you don't want to discuss it. We just met, so you have no reason to trust me with your secrets."

"What makes you think I have secrets?"

She smiles, and her cheeks dimple. "It's dead obvious, Gavin."

"Right. It would be. I'm good at being stoic, but hiding things never works out for me. I guess that's why my ex-wife left me." I stop dead, staring at empty space, as a chill sweeps over me. Why in the hell did I blurt that out? *I guess that's why my ex-wife left me.* I couldn't have sounded more pathetic if I'd started crying. "Uh, sorry. I shouldn't have said that. Just came out. Kinda ruins my image, doesn't it?"

"Oh, tosh." Jamie turns toward me, though she keeps holding my hand. "Having a painful past doesn't make you less of a man. My brother Lachlan used to think the same way, but Erica helped him move past all of that rubbish. Everyone knows his ex-wife was a rotten cow. Rory's first wife was that way too."

"Really? Huh. I kind of assumed all your brothers were like Aidan, annoyingly happy and good with the ladies."

"Aye, Aidan is a sweet man. But even he had some issues. I shouldn't share that with you, though, since it's Aidan's story, not mine."

"I get that." I realize something she just said, and it triggers my curiosity. "Rory's first wife? How many does he have?"

"Three ex-wives. He needs to find a good woman, but he's too afraid to step into the romance waters again."

I smirk. "He's probably worried a giant shark will eat him."

"So now lasses are sharks?" Jamie wags a finger at me and tsks. "Dinnae be a sexist, Gavin. I won't let you kiss me if you do."

Did she just suggest she might let me kiss her? Sounded that way. Damn, I want to kiss her so badly that I can almost taste it. I'd love to taste her, for sure. But I know she was joking.

I clasp her hand. "Let's keep walking while I tell you a little bit about me."

"You don't have to do that."

"I know. But I'd like to tell you, if you're comfortable with that."

"Of course."

We start ambling again, which is something I can honestly say I've never done before. Walking, sure. Hiking too. But never ambling. It feels good to be with someone who has no preconceived expectations and just wants to spend time with me.

Might as well dive into the shark-infested waters. "Before I can tell you about my ex-wife, Leanne, you need to understand what happened before my parents died. Calli is eight years younger than me, but she wound up taking care of me. That was later on, though. First, you should know that I joined the Marines straight out of high school, though I never imagined I'd wind up in combat. I wanted to serve my country, that was all. But I wound up getting deployed to Afghanistan."

Jamie holds my hand more firmly, but she doesn't speak.

"I, um, met Leanne..." My voice trails off, and I can't seem to convince my brain to let me say anything else. Memories of Afghanistan replay in my mind, showing me all the horrors in vivid detail. I stop walking and shut my eyes. "Can't talk about this. I'm sorry, Jamie."

"No need to be sorry. We hardly know each other, so it's none of my concern."

"Maybe we should go back to the house. I'm feeling wiped out all of a sudden."

Jamie doesn't complain or ask any questions. She just leads me back to the house. The puppies have even stopped bouncing around, like they can sense I'm not in a playful mood. I shouldn't get this way every time somebody mentions my military service, but I can't help it.

We walk back to the house faster than we had ambled away from it. That's not because Jamie wants to speed up. Once we reach the yard fence, I open the gate to let the puppies in, then shut it as Misty and Mandy race through the dog door into the house.

I grasp Jamie's upper arms. "Sorry about the sudden end to our nice little walk."

"No worries. I understand why you don't like to talk about your time in the Marines. I told you I have relatives and friends who have gone through similar things."

She's so damn sweet and empathetic that I need to make sure she understands. "I'm messed up, Jamie, and it's because of more than my military service or the fact that my marriage fell apart. My parents died five years ago, and I didn't handle it well. We just met, and I don't want you to get dragged down into my shit."

Jamie lays her palms on my chest. "That's my decision to make, not yours."

"I know. But—"

"Let me decide, Gavin."

I swallow hard and can't manage to say anything.

She moves closer with her body now inches away from mine. "Let's not discuss your past yet. I want to get to know you, but for now, I don't want to hear about your painful memories. We need to find out if we're compatible before we cross that bridge."

"You are a wonderful woman. Not sure I deserve you."

"I'm dead certain about that."

Her statement leaves me wondering whether she meant that she's positive I don't deserve her or that she believes I do deserve her. But like she said, we need to get better acquainted before we worry about that. She's gazing up at me with a serene expression, her hazel eyes glowing in the reflected sunshine, lighting up the green flecks in those irises.

I know I shouldn't ask, but…I can't help it. "Would you mind if I kissed you?"

"Not at all. I would love that."

How long has it been since I kissed any woman? Too damn long. I take hold of Jamie's upper arms and gently pull her closer until her body just barely touches mine. She tips her head back, exposing the slender column of her throat, and those hazel eyes shimmer with a deeper shade of brown, thanks to her pupils dilating. I could drown in those eyes and never want to be rescued.

She bites her bottom lip, releasing it so slowly.

I lower my head, brushing my nose against hers. Then I exhale a shallow breath and kiss her.

Jamie sags into me and fists her hand in my T-shirt. She exhales the sweetest little moan, and I tentatively slip my tongue between her lips. When she moans again, I take that as permission and push deeper into her mouth so I can coil my tongue around hers and tease the roof of her mouth with the tip. She wraps her arms around my waist. She must feel my dick hardening, but she doesn't shy away from that. Instead, she rocks her hips into me. I groan and delve deeper into her mouth, sliding my hands down to her ass.

"Dinner in five minutes!"

Though I hear those words, I can't understand the meaning or recognize who that is shouting at us. I go on kissing Jamie.

"Gavin! Jamie! Dinner in five minutes! If you don't get your butts in here, Aidan and I will eat everything, and you'll be grazing in the backyard with the squirrels."

Calli's voice finally penetrates my brain.

I reluctantly peel my mouth away from Jamie's lips. She seems a touch dazed, and I must look the same way. Kissing Jamie affected me like nothing else I've ever experienced before. I clear my throat. "Guess we'd better go into the house."

"Aye." That single syllable managed to convey everything I've been feeling too. "Aidan and Calli must have cooked for us. We wouldn't want to disappoint them."

I take Jamie's hand, leading her through the yard. As I reach for the handle on the sliding glass door, I pause to glance down at her. "Think I'd rather forage with the squirrels if it means I can kiss you more."

She grins. "I'd rather do that too."

But we head into the house instead. Sometimes being a mature adult really sucks.

Chapter Six

Jamie

In the morning, I wake up feeling so bloody fantastic that I almost can't believe I am awake. I must be dreaming, aye? There's no way Gavin actually kissed me, and that kiss absolutely could not have made me tingle and feel as if I might float away into outer space. But it did happen. I've kissed my fair share of men, but Gavin Douglas isn't just another lad. He's the sexiest, most virile, sweetest, and cleverest man I've ever known.

But, oh…that kiss.

I swear I can still taste him on my lips.

For a while, I simply lie here in my bed and revel in this feeling. I can't describe it, and I don't need to.

A knock rattles my door. "Rise and shine, Jamie. The rest of us are having breakfast, so if you want to eat, best get your erse out of bed."

"Haud yer wheesht, Aidan. I'll be there in a few minutes."

"Gavin might eat all the pancakes before you emerge from your cocoon."

"I need a shower first. So away and chew a brush, Don Juan."

My brother chuckles, and I hear his footfalls receding.

Aye, I essentially told him to sod off. Aidan was being bloody cheeky, so he can't blame me for cursing at him.

Ten minutes later, I walk out of my room having showered and dressed in record time. As I shuffle into the living room, I see Gavin and Aidan sitting on stools at the bar, chatting about who knows what while Calli watches them with an amused expression. Once I reach the kitchen area, I realize the men are discussing a very important subject.

Gavin smiles and winks at me, then slides an arm around my waist to pull me close. But he speaks to Aidan. "Come on, bro, you can't honestly believe that British soccer is better than American football."

"Americans don't play football. The rest of the world knows that the term football refers to the sport that involves a round ball that no one catches. They kick it about instead. Only American heathens call it 'soccer.' "

"Soccer is a sport for pansies. Try real football sometime, and we'll see how tough you really are. I'll even pay for your ticket so you can watch the Packers in action."

"Packers? Do you work in a factory?"

Gavin gives my brother a sarcastically disappointed look. "The Green Bay Packers. It's a football team."

"Isn't Green Bay in Wisconsin? I thought you were from Minnesota."

"Yeah, but I prefer the Packers. Just because I live in Minneapolis doesn't mean I'm required to support their team."

"How strange. If I decided to support Chelsea instead of Kilmarnock, I'd be run out of Scotland."

Gavin scrunches up his face. "What are Chelsea and Kilmarnock?"

"Football teams. Kilmarnock is in the Highlands."

"Uh-huh. Do you play so-called football?"

Aidan smirks. "Aye, but I prefer shinty."

Calli smacks two plates down on the bar, one for Aidan and one for Gavin. "Stuff your faces, boys. We girls are sick of listening to you two gab about sports. Aren't we, Jamie?"

"Oh, aye, we are."

Calli offers me a plate and a glass of orange juice, then she and I sit on the sofa to enjoy our breakfast and chat about much more interesting topics. We haver about how silly men are about sports as well as what we'd like to do today. The men don't seem to pay any attention to our conversation—until we begin to discuss what we should do today.

"Aidan and I should take you two on a tour of the Keweenaw Peninsula," Calli suggests. "The scenery is just gorgeous this time of year."

My brother crosses his arms over his chest as he turns his attention to Calli. "Why dinnae we let Gavin and Jamie go sightseeing on their own."

I can't help laughing. "Desperate to have a poke, eh?"

"*Falbh a ghabhail do ghnùis airson cac.*"

Gavin lifts one brow. "And for those of us who don't speak Gaelic, that means…"

"Away and take your face for a shite."

The man who kissed me yesterday, and did it so thoroughly that I'm still weak in the knees, gives Aidan a hard stare. It's pure sarcasm, though. "Don't speak to a lady that way, asshat."

I kiss Gavin's cheek. "Dinnae worry about me. I can handle any of my brothers, even all three at once."

"Yeah, I'm sure you can."

Aidan glances down at Gavin's arm, the one wrapped around my waist. His lips pucker briefly, then he sighs. "Let's go sightseeing. Dinnae want to leave you two alone, since I dinnae want to walk in on you two snogging. Actually, I don't want that to happen when I'm not in the vicinity either. So just dinnae touch my sister at all."

Does Aidan think I haven't kissed Gavin yet? He knows full well that I am not a virgin, yet he keeps talking about me as if I'm an innocent wee lassie. I still remember the day I bumped into Aidan at a chemist's shop, and he realized I'd been about to buy a box of condoms. I think he nearly had a heart attack then.

The four of us jump into Aidan's car, which Lachlan had hired for him without Aidan's consent. It's a lovely convertible, so we put the top down to get the best view of the surroundings. Despite the suggestion that we would go sightseeing, we end up simply visiting a few shops in the nearby villages. Not that I mind. As long as Gavin is with me, I'm happy to browse the silly trinkets and postcards on display in the shops.

Aidan and Calli pretend to be browsing a different section of the shop, but their plan is dead obvious. They want to keep an eye on us while pretending not to do that. Aidan is a bad liar and a bad actor. Calli isn't much better.

Gavin leads me over to a display of socks and taps his finger on one pair. "I think your brother Rory would love these."

"Do you? Why is that? Since you haven't met Rory, I'm curious about your reasoning."

"You mentioned that Rory is known as the Ogre of Loch Fairbairn. That sounds like he's probably a Bigfoot in disguise." He taps the package of socks again. "And these must have been modeled after him."

I take a good look at the socks and can't help smiling. "There are several variations of these. Which one do you claim must be a depiction of my brother?"

Gavin crooks his thumb under his chin and taps one finger on his mouth. "It's probably the socks that show a Bigfoot being abducted by aliens."

"I must have overlooked that one."

He snatches a pair of socks off the rack and holds it out to me. "Here you go. Rory would love these, I'm sure."

Laughter splutters out of me, and other customers give me strange looks. But I dinnae care. I accept the socks and study the image on them. It does indeed show a spaceship beaming a light down on a Bigfoot. I thrust the socks at Gavin and feign being offended. "If you gave these to Rory, he'd hurl you all the way around the globe and back again."

"Damn. He's that strong, huh? Well, maybe I should pick a different gift for him. We could give Lachlan the socks."

"You would do better to give them to Aidan. He loves jokes."

"I have noticed that." Gavin leads me over to a different display, one that showcases novelty mugs. "Oh, yeah, this is definitely more Rory's style."

Laughter bursts out of me again, garnering more odd looks that I ignore. "You think the Steely Solicitor wants a cup that's painted with neon colors? Pink, blue, yellow, orange. Oh, aye, that's Rory's style."

"I thought so." He snags a scarf off another display and slings it around his neck. "See? If it looks good on me, it'll be Rory's style for sure."

"Aye, because you two have so much in common—never having met or spoken to each other." This time I struggle to restrain my laughter and partially succeed. "Neon shades flatter you, Gavin."

"Don't they? I look hot in anything, though." He snatches up a pink hat. "See? I was right."

He is adorable when he's playful. I can't stop myself from leaning into Gavin and gazing up at him with what must look like adoration. No man has ever done silly things just to make me smile, and no one else has ever made me feel so good.

Gavin decides against buying all but one of the trinkets. He insists on giving me the Bigfoot UFO socks.

I clasp them to my chest and flutter my lashes. "Oh, thank you, Gavin. I will cherish these and wear them every day."

"Yeah, Rory ought to love that."

When and if Gavin ever meets my brother, I might need to make sure Rory has drunk half a bottle of whisky first.

Gavin does buy the neon-colored mug—for Aidan. My youngest brother grins and thanks Gavin profusely, and also sarcastically. I show Aidan my new socks, and he sighs, telling me that I risk developing an incurable disease called Conspiracy Theory-itis if I continue to fraternize with an American.

"You'll catch it too," Gavin tells Aidan. "You're fraternizing with an American, you know—my baby sister."

"No, Calli is immune. The disease only affects former US Marines who are flirting with my sister."

"Ah, so it's one of those bioengineered things. You should write a paper on it for a medical journal."

Calli and I start walking out of the shop, and the men trail after us while continuing to exchange sarcastic comments. By the time we get back to Calli's house, it's lunchtime. I am unusually hungry. I reckon visiting kitschy shops takes more out of a person than it seems like it should. Having fun is tiring, but in a good way. We enjoy our afternoon meal in the backyard while sitting at the picnic table. Gavin and I are on one side with Calli and Aidan directly across from us. Aye, the meal includes a fair amount of teasing and laughter.

Once the meal is over, Aidan makes a bizarrely sudden announcement. "Calli and I are going for a drive. Alone."

Gavin aims a hard stare at my brother. "I'm watching you."

Aidan glances at me, then returns his attention to Gavin. "Got my eye on you too."

Though my brother attempted to look tough when he spoke those words, he couldn't pull it off. It's just not in his nature. I know he was teasing Gavin, anyway.

Aidan clears his throat. "We will be away overnight. Please do not destroy Calli's home in the meantime. You'll need to care for the puppies too."

I salute. "Aye-aye, Captain Don Juan."

He squints at me. "There will be no *coinbheineadh* while I'm away, and absolutely no *feis*. Dinnae want you to catch *olcas*."

"Aidan! *Mhac na galla*. This is beyond the pale. You're behaving like Rory would in this situation, assuming I'm a brainless bairn who needs to be told what not to do."

"Sorry." Aidan winces. "I suppose I am going a wee bit too far."

We all carry the remnants of our meal back into the house, then Aidan and Calli grab their bags and drive away in the car Lachlan had hired.

That means Gavin and I are alone. Completely alone.

We settle onto the sofa, side by side but without touching each other. I reckon we're both slightly nervous about being genuinely alone together for the first time.

He stretches his arm out across the sofa's back, turning slightly toward me. "What were those things Aidan said to you? The stuff that made you so mad."

"Aidan told me he doesn't want us to fondle each other, and that we should not have sex." I compress my lips and shake my head. "But then he added that he's worried I might get gonorrhea from having a poke with you."

Gavin's expression goes blank for a few seconds. Then he laughs with such enthusiasm that a wee bit of spittle sprays from his lips. "No wonder he said some of that stuff in Gaelic. I would've needed to pummel him if I'd known what it all meant. A gentleman defends a lady's honor."

"That's the sweetest threat I've ever heard."

He shimmies a wee bit closer and rests his arm over my shoulders. "Let's not talk about your brother or my sister for a while. We can pretend we're all alone on a deserted island, and we can do anything we want."

The way his voice grew softer and deeper makes my body awaken, setting off a tingle that spreads out and becomes a warm, liquid feeling. That sensation dives deep under my skin. I pull in a ragged breath, exhaling it as we gaze deep into each other's eyes. His pupils have grown larger, darkening his beautiful brown eyes. *Bod an Donais,* I want him like mad, want him more than I ever imagined I could want any man.

I unconsciously lick my lips as my gaze lands on his mouth. I suck in another ragged breath, but I can manage only a shallow one this time. My focus drops to his lap, and I swear I can see his cock thickening before my eyes into a bulge the grows rapidly. I gulp but can't get rid of the lump in my throat.

Gavin licks his lips, just like I had done. "Want dinner now? Or should we skip ahead to dessert?"

Oh, aye, I know what he means. The rough tone of his voice elicits a delicious desire that sets off a slick heat between my thighs. "Skip straight to dessert, please."

His mouth slides into a sensual grin. "Can't deny a lady what she wants."

Chapter Seven

Gavin

I trace my fingertips over her skin, and I can tell her nipples are stiffening. I raise my other hand to brush my thumb across her lips. "I loved kissing you yesterday, but I want a lot more than that. I've never been this attracted to a woman I just met. Something about you makes me want to hold you and kiss you and make love to you, consequences be damned."

Jamie rotates toward me the slightest bit, and her knees brush against mine. "Dinnae care about the consequences either. Aidan might not approve, but he's not my keeper. I'm a grown woman who wants to be made love to."

"By anyone in particular?"

"You, of course." I settle my hand on her thigh, then move it down until I reach the hem of her skirt. It's the same skirt she wore this morning during our shopping trip and all day after that. "I want to touch you, Jamie, right now. I'll take it slow, so I can feel every inch of your soft skin and watch your reactions to my touch."

"Please touch me that way. I'm aching to feel your skin on mine."

My breathing has become labored, simply because I crave this woman so intensely. "I bought condoms in that little shop where we picked out gifts for everybody. I was hoping you'd want what I want, but I never imagined your brother would leave us alone together like this."

"He wanted to shag Calli in private. I doubt Aidan bothered to think about anything else, and in the morning, he'll probably realize that he left me alone with you, the American wolf."

I wink. "I'm a Marine, ma'am, not a wolf."

"Stop talking and make love to me."

"Yes, ma'am."

I push my hand up her inner thigh, under her skirt, and suddenly realize she isn't wearing any nylons. That doesn't shock me. But when I move my hand higher, I get a real surprise. "No panties, eh? I thought you were a good girl."

"Why would ye think that? I'm letting a man I barely know touch me intimately, and I fully expect that you'll ravish me very soon."

"Absolutely." I cup her groin, feeling her wetness trickle onto my skin. "For the record, I love a good girl who goes bad in the bedroom."

While I pet her folds, she sags against the sofa and lets her lids drift half closed. I press my lips to hers and kiss her deeply, groaning when she curls her hand around my dick, massaging it through my jeans. "Unbutton your shirt for me, please. I don't have enough hands."

Jamie does what I asked, then arches her back to show off those gorgeous tits. They aren't large, but just the right size to fit in my palm—if I didn't have both my hands occupied right now. Well, I might not have a free hand, but I've got a mouth. So, I duck my head to latch on to her nipple and suckle it gently.

She gasps, throwing her head back.

I push a finger inside her, feeling all that hot, slippery cream coat my skin. I can smell the scent of it too, and that makes me hunger to taste her. Can't wait one second longer. While she arches her back and her mouth falls open, I slide off the sofa to kneel between her legs. I grasp the waistband of her skirt and drag it down her thighs little by little. She writhes and grips the back of the sofa. I toss her skirt away, not giving a damn where it lands, and shove her thighs apart so I can push my head between them and latch on to her clit.

The flavor of her makes me groan even more deeply than before.

I tease her nub with my front teeth until she cries out again, then start licking her folds fiercely, devouring every bit of her cream while she grasps my head with both hands and her knees curl up as if she's about to come.

Then I thrust a finger inside her, and she goes off. The spasms of her inner muscles try to milk my finger, but her sheath is too small. So, I shove two more fingers in there while I keep suckling her clit and those muscles clench my fingers over and over. Once she's done, she slumps and closes her eyes. Her lips relax into a satisfied smile, but I am still not done yet.

"Ready for more?" I ask. "If you're wiped out, I can go into the bathroom and finish myself off."

I start to rise, but she sets one leg on my shoulder to stop me.

Her eyes fly open. "No, Gavin, you will not finish yourself off."

"Then you want me to fuck you right here on the sofa."

She shakes her head. "Not yet. I want you to sit on the coffee table and pull your jeans down to your ankles."

Do I comply? You're damn straight I do. Jamie gives the sexiest orders.

I sit on the cool, smooth surface of the coffee table and wait to find out what Jamie wants to do to me. The sweet Scot kneels between my legs, then bends forward, positioning her mouth directly in front of my stiff dick.

No, she won't do *that*. Will she? We just met a couple of days ago, so she couldn't want to...

She takes my dick into her mouth, coiling her tongue around the crown.

"Fuck, Jamie..."

The hottest woman I've ever met clasps the base of my erection and pumps from both ends, sucking me off like nobody's business. I grip the table's edge hard enough to cause pain, but I don't care about that. When her hair falls over my lap, it tickles my skin and especially my dick.

I gasp. "Damn, Jamie, you'll give me a heart attack if you keep doing that."

She ignores what I said and begins to massage my inner thigh with her soft fingers. I'm breathing so hard that my ears start to ring, and I'm almost hyperventilating.

Jamie pulls away. "Want to shag now?"

"Hell yeah." I pick her up and rise. But when I try to walk, I almost fall over. "Whoops. Forgot I still have my pants around my ankles."

She smiles. "And you have your shoes on."

I glance down. "Shit. Gimme a minute to take care of this, uh, issue."

Jamie keeps on smiling while I set her on the sofa and fix my wardrobe malfunction. She doesn't seem like she's mocking me, though. Jamie acts like she thinks my problem is cute and slightly entertaining. My erection flaps around while I remove my jeans and shoes. Maybe that's what she thinks is funny. I have just enough wits leftover to remember to dig a condom packet out of my jeans pocket.

Now completely naked, I spread my arms. "Armed and ready for action."

"But I was enjoying the striptease. Get dressed again and perform your show more slowly this time."

"No can do. I'll pop my cork if I have to touch my own dick again to get it stuffed inside my jeans."

She taps her chin, pretending to consider the situation. "Then I suppose you should fuck me now."

Oh, thank goodness. Don't think I could wait much longer. I scoop her up again and glance around. "Where should we do it?"

"My room."

"Yes, ma'am. I'd salute, but that probably would make me drop you."

She has her arms looped around my neck, but now she rests her cheek on my chest. Jamie looks even sweeter while cradled in my arms with no skirt or panties on and her blouse hanging open. She had already been barefoot when we sat down on the sofa. I glance at her cute little toes, with their pink-painted nails, and seeing them oddly makes me need to fuck her immediately and as hard as possible.

Jamie tickles the nape of my neck. "Shouldn't you be doing something, Gavin?"

"What? Oh, yeah, sorry."

I head for the smaller bedroom, the one where Jamie has been sleeping. The door to the master suite is open. Normally, when I get a glimpse of that room, I get a pit in my stomach because I know my sister has been sleeping in there—with a Scottish guy she met less than two weeks ago. But the second I walk into Jamie's room, I forget all about that. I've never told anyone that I feel a twinge of anxiety when I think about my sister shacking up with Aidan MacTaggart.

But can't complain about it. Calli is happier than I've ever seen her, and that's because of Aidan.

I use my foot to push the covers out of the way, then gently lay Jamie down on the sheets. She starts to sit up, so she can remove her blouse, but I shake my head. She relaxes and lets me slide that shirt off. Jamie doesn't even complain when I toss the blouse away and it lands on a chair by the window.

For a moment, I just gaze at her naked body and the way the moonlight coming in through the window paints her skin with its pale shades. She looks like a goddess from ancient mythology, lying in wait for her lover. That would be me. So, why am I just standing here gawking at her? *Make love to her, you moron, right now.*

I climb onto the bed, straddling her body.

Her smile has softened, and now it's imbued with sensual overtones. I bend my head to kiss her softly, slowly, while my dick nudges her belly and she runs her hands up my arms. A faint moan whispers from her lips. I grab the condom I'd tossed onto the bedside table and cover myself with it. Jamie tries to help me, but I wave her hand away. If she touches my dick, I'll explode—and it'll take too damn long for me to recover enough to make love to her.

"You are so damn beautiful, Jamie. I love kissing you, and I love gorging myself on your cream."

I press my lips to her throat, then paint a trail down her skin straight to her belly button, where I flick my tongue inside her navel to tease her. She moans, her breaths coming faster and shallower. I nuzzle her mound before I kiss my way back up to her tits. The areola is as rosy red as her stiff peaks, and I can't resist taking all her nipple into my mouth so I can scrape my teeth over it and suckle the tip.

Jamie spreads her legs, inviting me to take her body.

"Not just yet," I murmur. "Got another idea first."

She smiles in that sexy way I love, and I know that means she wants whatever I want.

I rise to my knees. "Push your tits together for me, but not too tightly."

Jamie's brows lift, but she does what I said.

I grasp the headboard, leaning over her body, and thrust my dick between those gorgeous tits. She seems a little confused, but she gets the picture once I start pumping my hips, pushing my dick between her breasts the way I would fuck her. The moisture on my crown rubs off on her skin, and the very tip pokes out just below her breastbone.

She bites her lip. "Och, Gavin, you're making me so randy that I might come without you even shagging me."

"I *am* shagging you. But don't worry, this is only the appetizer."

While I speed up the pace, she makes little moaning grunts that get me even hotter for her. My dick throbs. If I don't fuck her the usual way very soon, I might spew all over her chest and throat. The thought of that steals my breath, but I don't want to go off like that the first time we have sex.

I pull away and crawl backward until I'm in position.

Jamie massages her tits, arching her back slightly.

She seriously wants to kill me with her sexiness, and that's fine by me. Since she still has her thighs spread for me, I slide my hands under her ass to lift it off the bed just enough to give me the perfect angle. Then I ease my cock inside her, doing it so gradually that my pulse accelerates and pounds in my ears, while Jamie clenches her pillow above her head and arches her back even more. Once I'm seated as deep inside her as I can get, it's time to let go.

I pull back, then thrust into her hard. I keep thrusting, deeply and powerfully, making the bed frame creak and the legs thump. Jamie wraps her thighs around me while I pick up the pace, grunting and gasping, lifting her thighs higher to go deeper. She thrashes her head while shouting things that might be words, but I can't understand any of it. Maybe it's in Gaelic. I know I'll come any second, so I rub her clit to make sure she hits that peak first.

Jamie's entire body freezes. Her mouth falls open, but she seems incapable of making even the tiniest sound. Then her inner muscles clench around me in wave after wave of spasms. She cries out. I fuck her harder as electricity surges down my spine, barreling straight into my cock, setting off rapid-fire spasms. I couldn't stop if I wanted to, and I come so hard that I squeeze my eyes shut and can't breathe while I punch into her twice more, then collapse on top of the incredible woman who just let me pummel her body.

I roll off her, flopping onto my back. My breaths come in staccato gasps, and sweat has beaded on my brow. Sex had never been this good with anyone else. Maybe it's the forbidden aspect making it hotter. Her brother doesn't like me getting intimate with Jamie, so we're even. But this isn't about Aidan and Calli anymore. It's about me and Jamie and what we could be together.

Will we work out in the end? Only time will tell.

Chapter Eight

Jamie

We both lie on our backs, gradually catching our breath. I gaze up at the ceiling for a wee while, unable to make any muscle in my body function properly, not even my eyes. I have never before had a poke with a man I've known for a few days. If anyone had asked me a week ago if I would behave this way, I would have laughed at them. But Gavin makes me feel so good in every way possible.

Eventually, I regain the ability to move and turn onto my side to gaze at the man who gave me this delicious afterglow. "That was bloody brilliant, Gavin."

"I'm assuming that means you liked it."

"No, I didn't like it. I loved it." I sling an arm across his torso and kiss his chest, loving that I can taste the salty sweetness of his perspiration. "I would love to do that again."

He chuckles, though the sound is ragged and breathless. "Yeah, I'd love to do that too, but a man needs a break to recover between bouts of earth-shattering sex."

"I know you need time before we can shag again. So, why don't we eat something decadent and chat to each other in the meantime?"

"Now that's a 'bloody brilliant' plan."

A laugh bubbles out of me, and I can honestly say I have never laughed this way before. It's a cross between a giggle and a hiccup. Dinnae care if I sound ridiculous. I never want this feeling to end.

Gavin heads for the kitchen while I scurry into the bathroom. I needed to empty my bladder about thirty seconds before Gavin gave me a fantastic orgasm on the sofa, but I couldn't speak to tell him so once he put his mouth on my *brillean*. I should have taken a brief trip to the bog when he carried me into the bedroom, but I was too aroused to give a toss. That means now I desperately need to relieve myself. Once I've done that, I trot out into the living room and veer around the bar. Gavin is facing away from me, cooking something on the stove.

I come up beside him and sniff the air. "What are you making? It smells divine."

"French toast sticks, bacon, and scrambled eggs. I might not be a great chef, but I rock the breakfast foods—day or night." He pushes something around in the frying pan while keeping his attention exclusively on me. "I figured we both needed a boatload of protein."

"Oh, aye. Give me gobs of protein, please."

He glances at my body. "You're still naked."

"So are you."

Gavin smirks. "I wasn't complaining. But I figured you'd want to at least put on a robe. Women usually don't like prancing around buck naked outside of the bedroom, especially in front of sliding glass doors."

"Dinnae care what anyone thinks of me. Besides, we're in the back of beyond. Not many keekers out here, I imagine."

He freezes in the midst of scrambling the eggs. "What in the world is a 'keeker'?"

"Someone who spies on other people."

"Oh, you mean a peeping tom."

"That's what Americans call it, aye? My sister-in-law Erica has taught me some American expressions, and I taught her a few Scottish ones."

Gavin pours the egg mixture into a pan, glancing away from me only for a second or two. "Is Erica the only Yank you've ever met?"

"No, I've met the occasional American."

"And did you dislike them all?"

I kiss his bicep and smile up at him. "No, I love Yanks. They know how to shag a lass."

"Damn straight we do. And Scottish lasses know how to shag Americans."

This is the most unusual after-sex conversation I've ever had. Most men want to brag about their prowess, but they don't compliment me.

Calli's puppies had been asleep in the master suite when Gavin and I left the bedroom. Now, they come tumbling out of the hall. Misty and Mandy weave around our feet several times, then leap up to plant their paws on our bellies. I can't resist them. So, I bend my knees to let them lick my chin. Gavin ruffles their hair and scratches their heads, but he's busy cooking and can't play with the furry pair.

After a moment, the puppies both barrel out the dog door.

Gavin glances at me sideways and grins. "I love the way you laugh and smile whenever the puppies assault you."

"Cannae help it. They're adorable." I peer out the sliding glass doors. "Should we call them back in? It is dark outside."

"They'll come back in a minute, then we can shut the dog door."

By the time Gavin has finished cooking our meal, Misty and Mandy have returned to the house. He shows me how to close the dog door, then we sit down on the sofa to eat. Aye, we're still naked. We feed each other and tease each other, and we even shove food into each other's mouths. When a bit of syrup dribbles down my chin, a drop of it lands on my chest.

Gavin licks it away.

The puppies have kept us company. Misty has tucked herself behind Gavin's feet on the floor, while Mandy chose to snuggle up in the corner of the sofa. They're both sleeping, but I don't feel drowsy at all. Gavin suggests we should watch TV for a while to see if we get tired. If not, then we will "have some more fun under the sheets or on top of them," as Gavin tells me. He also suggests we might "get dirty on every surface in the house" because Calli and Aidan will never know how we defiled the premises.

I could fall for this man. He makes me feel…so bloody good.

After the meal is over, and the puppies have eaten the leftovers, Misty and Mandy retreat to the master suite. Gavin says they do that because they always sleep in Calli's room and it makes them feel safe when she's away. That leaves us, the only humans in the house, alone in the living room. We've agreed to remain in the nude. It just feels right.

We've been watching a documentary about the mating habits of tropical birds, only because we couldn't find anything else to watch. Neither of us likes reality shows. But the documentary about birds has an odd effect on Gavin.

He has his arm draped across my shoulders. But now, he dips his head to whisper into my ear, "Something weird is happening to me. Watching this show about birds is making me so fucking horny."

"Aye, me too. It's very strange."

"Maybe we feel this way because the narrator keeps using the word copulate."

"Hmm, that could be the reason." I rotate my head toward him, and our lips brush against each other. "Or maybe you are just a very, very naughty man who cannae stop thinking about sex."

"That's a good point. But I'm naughty only because you are so hot."

I smirk. "You're blaming me? I might need to punish you for that."

"Your willing slave will do anything you want."

"Want to make good on the suggestion that we should get dirty on every surface in the house?"

"Oh, yeah, baby. Let's do it." He nods toward the television. "Should we leave the raunchy bird documentary on?"

I grin. "Why not?"

"Just let me go grab another condom. Got at least one more in the pocket of my jeans." He squints as he surveys the living room. "Where'd I leave my pants?"

"We tossed our clothes into a pile over there." I point toward the far corner of the room. "Stay right where you are. I'll get a condom for you."

I race over to the pile of clothing. While I hunt about for his jeans, Gavin makes catcalls.

"Look at that fine Scottish ass," he calls out. "Just watching those round, sweet tits bouncing is getting me hard. This is a much better show than the one on TV."

Having located my prize, I decide to tease him the way does with me. But instead of making suggestive comments, I hold the condom packet between my teeth and crawl across the floor on my hands and knees, purposely swaying my hips and tossing my hair.

Then I kneel directly in front of Gavin, working my jaw to make the condom packet flap.

Gavin chuckles. "You're the cutest hot chick I've ever met."

I flutter my lashes, flapping the packet again.

He plucks it away, then taps the packet on my nose. "Maybe we should try mating the cockatoo way. Remember how the boy climbed on top of the girl, who was lying on her tummy?"

I shimmy forward and lay my hands on his thighs. "The boy cockatoo also shoves his beak up the lass's erse. Not sure I want you to do that to me. It looked painful, though the lass didn't seem to mind."

"Good point. We aren't cockatoos, but they have given me another idea." He pulls me onto his lap. "Wanna screw outside under the light of the moon?"

"Do you mean in the yard? Or in the woods?"

"The yard. Might be wolves out there in the dark."

I kiss him softly. "Thank you for worrying about my safety while we have a poke."

He wraps his arms around me. "I'll watch out for your safety all the time, baby."

I never used to like it when a man called me "baby." But every time Gavin says that, I melt inside and want to wrap my entire body around him. I would've expected a tough man like Gavin Douglas to avoid getting sentimental or saying sweet, loving things. Of course, my only role models for ex-military men are my cousins Logan, Magnus, and Munro. They are not average lads. None of them would behave the way Gavin does with me, though to be fair, I haven't seen my cousins with women. Maybe they do behave in the same manner.

No, I can't picture Magnus the bounty hunter cuddling with a lass.

Gavin sneaks down the hall to check on the puppies, but they're still happily sleeping. We leave the dog door shut while we go outside, barefoot, and search for the best spot for having a poke. After examining the entire yard, he selects a location at last.

And I laugh. "You needed ten minutes to choose the most dead-obvious place? You want to shag on the grass."

"Yeah. I considered other spots, but they all had something that wasn't right—like rocks sticking up out of the dirt or a lack of a soft surface." He slings an arm around my waist and tugs me close. "Can't have you getting scrapes or cuts."

"That is so sweet, Gavin. Thank you for worrying about my skin."

We do wind up making love on the soft, cool grass, beneath the big tree that provides shade in the daytime. A clear, moonlit sky sheds its milky light on us, so we can see each other almost as well as in the daytime. The moon is full, after all. Gavin lavishes light kisses over my entire body, arousing me tenderly until my breaths quicken and my heart races. By the time he pushes his cock inside me, I'm on the verge of orgasm. But he knows exactly how to keep me on the edge without letting me come until he's ready for us both to do that.

Making love has never been so literal. I've fallen for him here on the lawn with the moon above us. We created a bond with our bodies.

In the afterglow, we lie on the grass on our backs, holding hands while the moon gradually sinks lower and lower in the sky. We joke and tease each other, but we also discuss more serious things—like what we want our lives to become. I tell Gavin about my current state of unemployment and how I haven't yet found a long-term career path. He listens without commenting while I ramble on about my life.

"All my relatives have tried to help me find a job, and I know they mean well. But none of my positions have lasted longer than five years. I'm not a wastrel. I want to be settled in my life, but most of all, I want to find the right man and settle down to have children."

I glance at Gavin, expecting him to seem uncomfortable because of what I said. But he simply gazes up at the stars with a serene expression.

"Gavin, are you awake?"

He turns his head to look at me. "Yeah, I'm awake. And I heard everything you said, but I was waiting to find out if you had more to say."

"Aren't you ready to leg it? I did talk about my desire to start a family."

"Leg it? What does that mean?"

"To run away."

"Oh, I see." He rolls onto his side and drapes an arm across my belly. "Not going to leg it anywhere except back into the house. And for the record, I'd love to have kids. My ex-wife wasn't really into the idea."

"But we barely know each other. You should be horrified."

Gavin lays a hand on my cheek to turn my head toward him. Then he rubs his thumb across my bottom lip. "I care about you, Jamie. Care a lot. I know we just met, and I should be freaked out by how quickly we've gotten close. But I can't feel anything bad when I'm with you. It's all good, and that's something I've never experienced before."

"Neither have I. The only serious boyfriend I ever had seemed like Prince Charming, but he mutated into a slimy toad." I place my hand over his on my cheek. "But somehow I know you would never become a cretin like that chancer."

"Thanks. Maybe I should have a T-shirt printed up with that endorsement on it. 'This guy is not a slimy toad.' I could make a fortune selling those shirts."

I love his sarcastic sense of humor. I love everything about him, actually. He's never mean, but he enjoys making sly jokes. Whenever he softly kisses me, I feel a pang in my chest.

Oh, aye. I am falling for Gavin Douglas.

Chapter Nine

Gavin

Jamie insists on making breakfast for us in the morning, just to prove that she's capable of doing that. I never thought she wasn't. But I've realized lately that she feels kind of inferior to her brothers and sisters. Catriona is an archaeologist, Rory is a solicitor, Lachlan is a financial adviser, Fiona runs a dress shop, and Aidan owns a construction company.

Well, that's what I assume—until I notice something strange about her grammar. She started out using the present tense but then shifted into past tense when she talked about Aidan and Catriona.

"What gives?" I ask as we're snuggled together on the sofa, having stuffed our faces with Jamie's excellent food. "It sounds like Catriona and Aidan don't have jobs anymore. You used the past tense when you mentioned them."

"Aye, it's true. They are both…seeking new opportunities."

"They're unemployed. You can just say it. I won't think they're massive losers because they're between jobs."

"What do you do for a living?"

I squirm and wince. "Well, I, uh…It's nothing interesting."

"Please tell me, Gavin. I'm currently unemployed, like Aidan and Cat, so you don't need to feel embarrassed to tell me about your job—or your lack of one, if that's the case."

"Oh, I've got a job. It sucks, though." I scratch my cheek and wince again. "I'm a sales rep for a company that sells emergency home recovery services."

"What does that mean? I've never heard of that sort of thing, so I'm interested in learning more."

"You really don't want to know more. It's boring as hell."

Jamie has been smiling sweetly at me ever since we sat down on the sofa. She seems to genuinely want to know about my job, and I don't want to get cagey about that. I've avoided telling her a lot of things about my past, so the least I can do is share this boring part with her.

"Basically, I talk to people on the phone all day long. Mostly, it's cold calling where I harass perfectly nice people and try to talk them into buying services they don't need. About sixty percent of my job is like that."

She just keeps on gazing at me like I'm Superman.

"But I do also work with customers who've experienced a residential disaster and call us for help. That's what the company calls it. Residential disasters. It means that if your sewer backs up or your septic system goes wonky, we're here for you. We also handle broken water pipes, mold problems, insect infestations, and other stuff."

Jamie studies me for a moment. "You expected me to be disgusted with your job, didn't you?"

"Yeah. Duh. I annoy people for a living."

"But you also give people the services they need in an emergency. I assume the company actually delivers on their promises and doesn't simply take the money and not do the work."

"No, our disaster recovery team does the work, and they always finish the job." I think my whole face is scrunching up now. And yeah, I'm using my baby sister's term for that expression. "But lately, most of what I do is cold calling. I hate that."

"Have you looked for another job?"

"Yeah. The job market is tight these days. Hard to find anything I'm qualified for."

"But you must have had other sorts of jobs in the past."

I slump against the sofa and sigh. "My only previous work experience was in the Marine Corps."

"Oh. But your job in the military must have given you some experience that you could leverage in the civilian world."

"My MOS was ground ordnance maintenance."

She bites one side of her lip. "What does that mean? I'm not well-versed in military jargon."

"MOS means military operational specialty. Basically, my specific job in the Corps which was ground ordnance maintenance. That means I inspected, repaired, and maintained weapons systems in the field." I let my head fall back against the sofa. "So you see, I don't have relevant experience for getting a civilian job. The only thing I could get was being a telemarketer." I snort. "And I only got that gig because the guy who interviewed me liked my voice. He said it would make people feel more at ease."

"Aye, that's a fact. I feel at ease whenever I'm with you." She kisses my cheek. "And you do have a lovely voice."

"Uh, thanks. I guess. My boss would agree with you, apparently."

"I've embarrassed you, haven't I? Sorry."

"Don't apologize. But no, I'm not embarrassed. I appreciate any compliments you want to give me, though I'll admit I'm not great at accepting things like that. Just not sure I deserve it."

She snuggles up to me and splays a hand on my chest. "I can think of several compliments I could give you that would probably make you blush."

"Doubt it. But it might be fun to let you try."

"That sounds like an invitation."

"Because it is. Do your best to make me blush."

She slides a hand up my inner thigh while giving me a sly smile. "You'll have to do better than that, Jamie."

"All right." She swings her leg over my thighs to squat on my lap. "Just wait, *gràidh*. I'll have you blushing soon."

"What did you just call me?"

"*Gràidh*. It means 'darling' in Gaelic."

"Thanks, baby. I love being called 'darling.' But I'm still not blushing, so you might as well give up and—"

Jamie thrusts a hand down to my groin, cupping my dick through my jeans, then she begins to massage me. "You gasped."

"Yeah. That's what happens when you take my dick in your palm, but it doesn't mean I'm embarrassed."

She puckers her lips and releases my dick. "I'll need to think on the problem for a wee bit longer."

"Your determination is cute." I move her off my lap, then pull her close. "Forget about making me blush. Let's make out instead."

Jamie grins. "That's a dead brilliant idea."

"When do you think Aidan and Calli will come home?"

"They didn't say. But it's nearly ten o'clock, so they might be back at any moment."

"No time to waste, then." I turn toward her and rest my arm across the sofa's back, then use my other arm to pull her firmly against my chest. "Time to make out."

We tip our heads toward each other at the same time, and we keep our eyes open for a few seconds after our lips meet. I've never kissed a woman this way before, but I love gazing into her hazel eyes from such close proximity. I can count every line in her irises and watch as her pupils dilate, darkening her eyes. Mine must be doing the same thing. Then we both shut our eyes at the same instant.

I grasp her hip while she thrusts a hand into my hair to cradle the back of my head. Our tongues thrust and tangle with each other. Her hair tickles my cheek. My pulse revs up, and my dick starts to thicken. I know kissing her will lead to screwing, and with my sister and her lover about to arrive at any moment, we should stop.

But I can't do it. Jamie tastes too damn good.

The front door bursts open.

Jamie and I both jump at the same time, tearing our mouths away from each other.

Aidan and Calli just walked into the house. My sister seems sheepish, but Aidan wears a thunderous expression that I didn't actually think the guy had in him. Well, I guess he does have a tough side after all. And seeing me kissing his sister brought it out in him.

Calli shuts the door and seizes Aidan's arm to stop him. He halts and glances at her sideways.

Jamie flings a hand up to cover her mouth, like she's trying to hide her swollen lips.

I pretend I have no idea what Aidan's upset about. Why? Just because. I'm sure Aidan "had a poke" with my sister several times last night, so I have every right to give him a hard time.

Calli aims her gaze at Don Juan. "Let's not overreact."

Strictly to maintain my I-don't-give-a-shit attitude, I get up and face my sister and her lover, with the sofa between us. "Hey, didn't think you'd be back so soon."

My sister rolls her eyes at me. "Duh. Figured you wouldn't be sucking face with Aidan's sister if you thought he was about to come home."

Aidan swerves his gaze to Calli and mouths, "Home?"

Her eyes flare wide. Her lips fall open. Her gaze flicks between me and the Scot.

Now I feel like punching someone—preferably a man with a Scottish accent. "You two are living together. I knew it."

"Not the way you mean. He sleeps here."

"With you."

"Honestly, we've already had this conversation." She tugs her shirt down, though it didn't need to be tugged. That's one of her tells. When Calli gets nervous because she's hiding something, she fusses with her clothes. "Aidan is not my boyfriend."

Aidan and I both snort and smirk at Calli. Hey, look at that. We finally agree on something. Jamie snorts and smirks too, though I wouldn't have expected that. She's on my side? I think so, which is kind of strange.

My sister lodges her hands on her hips and tries to scowl at us.

But we all glance at each other, nod, and then smile at Calli. Her shoulders slump, and her arms go slack.

Jamie springs off the sofa, clasps my hand, and puts on the biggest, brightest, phoniest smile—aimed at Calli. "Gavin's not my boyfriend either, then."

"Are all you Scottish people so snarky?" Calli asks.

Aidan throws an arm around her shoulders. "You like it. From me, at least."

Jamie looks at me, her smile becoming genuine. Then she faces Calli. "Would you mind if Gavin was my boyfriend?"

Calli's mouth falls open again, and I can tell she wants to say that yes indeed, she would mind. But my sister isn't stupid. And I'm sure she can tell how much I like Jamie. On top of that, Calli knows it would be hypocritical for her to demand that Jamie stop spending time with me when she's been shacking up with Aidan.

Surprisingly, he reaches that conclusion first. "It's all right. Let them have their fun."

I raise my brows. "Fun? I like Jamie a lot. It's more than a good time. Not like you and my sister, who've been having sex while she says you're not her boyfriend. At least I'm upfront about it."

Calli winces.

Aidan stiffens, narrowing his gaze. "Upfront? You snogged with my sister while I was away."

"You want I should do it in front of you?" I smirk. "All right, I will."

Then I drag Jamie into my arms and crush my mouth to hers. She dissolves into a human puddle, held up by my body. She moans a little, just enough to make my libido kick into high gear, and I struggle to tamp down my lustful instincts.

Aidan growls. Seriously, he does. "Why dinnae ye just tear her clothes off right in front of us?"

No, I would never embarrass Jamie like that. So, I release her. Jamie's cheeks have turned a sweet shade of rosy pink. She bites her lip and avoids looking at me.

Aw, shit. I *did* embarrass her. I hadn't meant to do that.

Calli rushes over to wrap an arm around Jamie's shoulders and pull her away from me. "Both of you, stop harassing the poor girl. Gavin, quit trying to annoy Aidan. And you Aidan, let your sister live her own life. At least she's not in Chicago trolling the clubs. My brother is a good man." She throws a reproving look at me. "Most of the time."

Aidan and I bow our heads. Yeah, we both behaved like asses. I peek up at Jamie, with my eyelashes as cover.

Then I hear her whisper something to Calli. "Will you be my honorary sister?"

"Wouldn't that make me Aidan's sister?"

"Not at all. But if you marry him, you could be my sister-in-law. Even better than honorary sister."

She glances at Aidan.

Don Juan blows out a big breath. "I'm sorry. Won't happen again."

I clear my throat. "Yeah, me too. Sorry."

Calli shakes her head at us. "I suppose we will accept your half-assed apologies."

Jamie glances at me and winks. "Aye, we will accept it."

I really, really want to make it up to Jamie. Not sure how to do that. But I can't leave without making things right with my sister.

She waves a hand at me, as if she read my mind. "Go. Take Jamie to dinner, make out with her in the car, whatever. You're adults, and we—" She aims a pointed look at Aidan—"will not interfere. Will we?"

"You have my word."

I walk up to my sister. "Calli, I am sorry for being such a jerk."

She gives me a slight smile. "I know you're sorry. Let's forget about it."

I claim Jamie's hand, leading her out the sliding glass doors. Once we're out of earshot and eyesight of Calli and Aidan, I stop to ask a question. "What would you like to do now? Go out to dinner? Have a picnic in the yard?"

"Would you show me that hunting cabin where you've been sleeping?"

"Sure thing. But it's not much of a cabin. There are no real amenities, just bare floors and a tiny bathroom. I've been bunking on the floor with just a sleeping bag. It's well-padded but still counts as roughing it."

"Dinnae care. I'd like to see it anyway."

"All righty, then."

We leave the yard and begin ambling down the path that leads to the cabin. But we keep glancing at each other at the same time, repeatedly, and smile too. Soon, we're picking up the pace, almost jogging in our zeal to get there and be alone again. I look at Jamie, and the way her hair flies around her face and her smile has become a brilliant grin, gives me a feeling I've never felt this strongly before.

I think I'm happy. And it's all because of Jamie.

Chapter Ten

Jamie

By the time we reach the cabin, we're both breathing so hard that we can barely speak. Maybe we hadn't needed to sprint all the way here. But we couldn't wait, so excited to be alone again that we would've run for miles to get here. Every time Gavin grinned at me, I felt as if my feet had lifted off the ground like helium balloons.

But we have a wee problem.

I study the structure before us. "This is the hunting cabin? It's in a tree."

"No, it's attached to the tree. Technically, it's a deer blind. But Calli told me that the guy who built this blind wanted more than a place to squat while he waited for deer to wander by so he could shoot them." Gavin waves up toward the wee structure. "He decided to live here too."

As I gaze up at the so-called cabin, I twist my lips into an expression that probably conveys my skepticism. "Are you sure the 'cabin' will hold us? It won't break and come crashing down on us? I dinnae care to become a human pancake."

"I would never let that happen to you." He clasps both my hands, facing me. "I've slept here since the day I arrived in Michigan, and I'm a lot heavier than you are. If this thing was in danger of collapsing, I wouldn't have brought you here."

"Aye, I know that. But I do have a slight issue with heights."

He chuckles, though the sound is full of affection. "Don't worry. I'll help you get up there. The cabin has stairs. They're around the side, where you can't see them."

"No ladder?"

Gavin shakes his head and makes a cross shape over his heart. "My word of honor."

I let him lead me around the side of the cabin. It does indeed have a set of stairs that lead up to the main part of the structure. But we do need to climb up through a sort of hatch in the floor to access the wee shack. Gavin gives my erse a shove with both hands. I appreciate the help, but I could have gotten in here without that. I'm sure he saw an opportunity to get his hands on my erse and couldn't resist.

Well, I might've done the same thing if he'd climbed in ahead of me. That man has a braw erse.

Once I've reached the top of the stairs and climbed in, I straighten and take in my surroundings. Aye, it is a genuine cabin. But I cannae admire the decor yet, not when Gavin just climbed in, and I got a fine view of his backside.

I sigh with mock wistfulness. "Och, Gavin, you do have a braw erse for sure. I could watch you crawling about on the floor for hours just to see those glutes flex."

He stands up and groans, rubbing his lower back. "Damn, climbing into this place always gives me a crick in my back."

"Would you like a rubdown?"

"Seriously?"

I nod.

His lips form a suggestive smile. "Yeah, I'd love that. Then I'll do the same for you."

"Undress, please."

He salutes. "Yes, ma'am."

While Gavin gets naked, I finally take in the full scope of the cabin. It has no living room or bedroom, only a single open space with a wee attached bathroom that is indeed quite small. I'm surprised Gavin can fit in there. The sleeping bag lies on the floor beside an oil lantern. The shack does have a kitchen, of a sort. If a body accepted that a wee wood stove can be a kitchen appliance too. Well, why not?

Gavin clears his throat deliberately.

I spin round to face him—and cannae help smiling in the same sly way he had done a moment ago. "You definitely look best starkers. You should become a nudist, so I can see you naked every day."

"Only if you do the same."

"Is that an order?"

"Yes, ma'am, it is."

I salute, then strip off my clothing faster than even I thought I could do it. Then I realize we have a problem. I hug myself and rub my arms. "It's a wee bit chilly in here."

"Shit. Sorry, I forgot to turn on the wood stove. Gimme a minute."

He excavates a throw blanket from his luggage and tosses it to me. While I sit cross-legged on the sleeping bag, he wraps the blanket around me. I pull my knees up to my chest, and he fires up the wood stove in record time.

Soon, warmth begins to fill the cabin.

Gavin kneels in front of me. "Bet I can warm you up a lot faster than a stove or a blanket."

"I'm dead sure you can." I toss the blanket away and lie down on the sleeping bag, on my back, stretched out in the middle. "Warm me up, Gavin."

He crawls onto our makeshift bed, straddling my body. His straight arms hold him up, so he's not actually touching me, not yet. "Would it freak you out if I said I'm falling in love with you?"

"No. I'm falling for you too."

He sits back on his heels and begins gliding his hands up and down my legs, taking it slow at first, then speeding up little by little. His motions create a delicious friction that arouses me and heats me up. By the time he moves his hands up to my belly, I'm already quite warm. He runs his palms over my entire torso, from my hips to my throat, all while carefully avoiding my breasts. The nipples had been taut from the cold, but now, they're stiff because this man knows how to turn me on so swiftly that it's breathtaking.

"Jamie, sweet Jamie. Wanna make love to you slowly this time."

"Please do. I love having a poke with you."

"Gotta say, I love Scottish slang. It's cute and dirty at the same time."

Suddenly, I experience a strong need to ask for something I've never wanted before. "Talk dirty to me, Gavin."

"Only if you call me Gav. That's my nickname, and I need to hear you calling me that while we fuck."

"All right, Gav. Talk dirty, please."

He molds his hands to my breasts and massages them slowly. "Feel free to beg all you want, baby."

I arch my back slightly, needing to feel his hands more firmly grasping my flesh. When he flicks his fingertip over my nipple, I gasp.

"You have the most beautiful tits in the world." He lies down beside me and resumes tracing his hands over my skin. "I'd love to pull one of those rosy peaks into my mouth and suckle until you start writhing. But I need to get you so turned on that your cream will be dribbling down your inner thighs."

"Oh, Gav, please do that."

He pets my mound, splaying his fingers through the hairs there. "Ah, fuck, Jamie. I can smell your cream now. Thought it would take longer, but you got wet right away. I love that about you. But I wanna see how drenched I can get you by using only my hands."

"Och, I'm begging you, do that to me."

Gavin glides his palms up and down my skin, covering every inch in slow increments. He begins with my throat, where he splays his fingers over my flesh and teases me with the tips. I wriggle and gasp. He drags that hand down my breastbone, all the way to the edge of my mound.

"Your skin is so damn soft, it's like silk." His voice has dropped to a husky murmur that makes me shiver a wee bit. "Need to spread your legs and push my head between them so I can lap up every little bit of your juices. I already know you taste like honey and cream and caramel."

Gavin slides his hand between my thighs but doesn't touch my folds or my mound. Instead, he runs his palm down one leg and back up the other, his touch so delicate that it heightens my desire even more. I'm almost shaking from the need to have him inside me.

"I changed my mind. Please fuck me now, Gav. Cannae stand this any longer, need you inside me."

"Oh, thank goodness. My dick's about to explode."

Though I successfully fight off the impulse to laugh at that statement, I can't stop myself from smiling. He seemed so relieved, and it was utterly adorable. But I won't tell him that. Not yet. Maybe after we shag.

But I do need to remind him of something. "Condom?"

"Shit, yeah, of course. Almost forgot again, didn't I?" He leaps up to find his clothes and get the condom. Then he joins me on the sleeping bag again, now straddling my body. "You are the most beautiful woman in the world. But more than that, you're the kindest, sweetest woman and one tough chick when it comes to dealing with your brother. You are amazing, Jamie."

Gavin lowers himself onto his elbows, placing his body in full contact with mine. He carefully avoids crushing me with his heavier weight. Then he begins to slide his length inside me little by little, brushing his lips across mine and exhaling his heated breath over my mouth. The friction of his skin against mine makes my heart beat faster even while his leisurely movements relax me. It seems contradictory, yet it's what I feel. No man has ever made love to me like this.

No one except Gavin.

I glide my hands up and down his back while I spread my thighs to give him more room. He gazes into my eyes unwaveringly, and I gaze into his in the same way. It's a sort of connection I've never experienced before, and I love it. I bend my knees, grazing my nails up and down his back as I lift my hips in a gentle rhythm to push his cock deeper inside me. Gavin groans deeply, his eyes drifting half closed. I close my eyes too, so I can revel in every sensation. I've grown even wetter with every passing second, so much so that I can hear the faint sucking sound as he takes my body.

He scrunches up his face. "Wanted to go slow, need to go faster."

"Anything you need. Just do it."

Gavin raises onto his straight arms and starts pumping into me with more force, though he still keeps the pace measured. Moment by moment, inch by inch, he speeds up his thrusts. I grip his biceps and lock my ankles behind his erse, holding on while he punches into me harder and faster until my body begins to slide up and down on the flat surface.

Wild, incoherent cries tumble from my lips.

He grits his teeth, and his lips peel back, as if he needs to come so badly that it hurts. I feel the same desperate need for release. With his cock pummeling me, I can't stop my body from pushing me over the edge. A long, keening cry spills from my lips and gradually rises in pitch and volume until it becomes a shrill scream. My inner muscles pulsate around him as I come, and suddenly, I've lost my voice. Can't breathe either. As he pounds into me a few more times, letting out harsh yells in time with his thrusts, I suddenly regain my voice enough to release a single cry.

"Gavin!"

Then we both collapse. He falls on top of me, but immediately shifts about as if he means to roll off my body.

I wrap my arms round him. "Dinnae move yet. I love the weight of you on top of me."

"Okay, I'll stay put. Let me know if I get too heavy for you."

"Gavin, you are the sweetest man in the world."

We spend the remainder of the day inside this wee cabin, naked for the entire time, while we chat and laugh and generally bask in the afterglow of incredible sex as well as our newly forged bond. I've never felt this deeply for any man, not even the ones I dated for several months. Gavin Douglas is not like anyone else, and I know I never want to say goodbye to him.

After our third round of hide-and-go-seek, during which Gavin pretended to hide under an invisible bed, we decide it's time to return to Calli's house. Gav looked bloody ridiculous when he curled up as if he actually were under a bed. I laughed so hard that my eyes watered. And when he crawled out of his supposed hiding place, he acted as if he had bumped his head on the imaginary bed frame.

And I laughed even harder.

We stroll back to the house hand in hand, glancing at each other often, smiling in the way couples in love do. I've seen that happen with other people, but never with me. Not until I met Gavin. Now everything has changed, and I'm beginning to see a future with him, unfolding from this moment on.

As we walk through the sliding glass doors, I sense that something isn't right. We both halt just inside the doorway, exchanging confused glances. Aye, he must feel the difference too. What is it, exactly?

"The puppies aren't bounding around," Gavin says. "I don't hear any noises at all in here. Aidan and Calli should be talking while Mandy and Misty try to slather their tongues all over them."

"Aye, something is different. I feel it too."

He grips my hand more firmly as we shuffle across the living room.

Calli and Aidan emerge from the hallway. Their expressions prove our suspicions were correct. Calli seems completely forlorn, while Aidan wears a stoic mask. I have never seen my brother look that way. Never.

"What's happened?" I ask.

"Pack your things," Aidan tells me. "We're going home first thing tomorrow."

I gawp at him. "Home? I don't want to leave yet. If Calli's going with you, then Gavin should come with us too."

"You and I are flying home. Calli and Gavin will stay here."

"But—"

"No arguments. Go pack your things—now."

Gavin's hand has tightened around mine so much that it almost hurts. He aims his steely stare at Aidan. "Tell us what's going on. We deserve that much."

Aidan sighs, and his shoulders sag. "Aye. Let's all sit down, and I'll explain everything."

Chapter Eleven

Gavin

I lead Jamie over to the sofa while Aidan and Calli sit in arm-chairs positioned at opposite sides of the sofa. They don't look at each other, except for the occasional furtive glance. The last time I saw my sister looking so dejected had been right after our parents died in a car crash. Now, Aidan and Calli explain everything to us.

Calli has a husband she never told me about. I knew she'd been friends with a guy called Rade back in college, but now I learn that he tricked my baby sister into marrying him so he could get a green card. That's marriage fraud, and he's held it over her for years. I never had a clue. After my time in Afghanistan, and our parents' deaths, I'd been useless. Calli's dilemma is my fault.

"No, Gavin, it's not your fault," Calli insists. "I made my own mistakes and believed the wrong man."

"But I should've been there for you. Instead, I made you handle all the funeral arrangements and deal with the life insurance company. I'm your big brother, and I failed you."

I can tell Calli wants to argue with me, to convince me I'm wrong. But she must realize now isn't the time for that. She keeps quiet.

Aidan tells us about his rock-climbing accident, and how the girl he'd taken up a big mountain with him had nearly died in the rockslide that injured them both. She suffered the most severe wounds, though. He blames himself, of course, just like I blame myself for Calli's dilemma. Seona, the woman who was involved in the accident, now claims she's pregnant with Aidan's child. That's why he and Jamie need to go home.

Though I want to argue about that, I realize Aidan is upset about the Seona situation. He wants to take Jamie home with him because he needs to be with his family. I get that. But the thought of Jamie flying away from me makes my chest ache and my throat tighten. She means more to me than a casual fling. I want to spend the rest of my life with her.

We all try to sleep that night, but given our haggard expressions in the morning, I know none of us managed to get any rest. Breakfast becomes a silent movie. Might as well have turned the world into black and white. Jamie and Aidan spend most of the morning packing up their suitcases and stowing them in the trunk of Aidan's rented Mustang. Then they spend a while arguing out in the yard while Calli and I sit on the sofa, at opposite ends, watching them.

Jamie doesn't want to leave. I can tell that much just from watching her argue with Aidan.

Though I make lunch for all of us, we don't eat much. We avoid looking at each other too.

Now, it's time for Jamie and Aidan to leave.

Calli needs to say goodbye to him alone, and I get that. So, I lead Jamie out of the house. We halt beside the Mustang.

She clasps my hands. "Dinnae want to go."

"And I don't want you to go either. But your family needs you, and I've gotten to know you well enough that I can say with absolute certainty that you will never forgive yourself if you aren't there when Aidan needs you." I brush my thumb over her cheek. "He's your best friend. You told me that."

"You're right, I know. But I..." She raises onto her toes to look straight into my eyes. "I love you, Gavin."

"I love you too. And we will see each other again, that's a promise."

Aidan shambles out of the house, looking as dejected as I feel. He hides it pretty well, but guys can tell when one of our buddies is upset. We might not want to talk about it, but we can tell. Women aren't the only ones with insight into the human condition.

I give Jamie a quick, soft kiss. "I won't forget about you, not ever. You're the only one for me, and I'll fight for us. However long it takes, I'll wait."

Jamie and Aidan climb into the car.

I stand here watching while the only woman I've ever really loved rides out of my life. A hard pang hits me in the chest, and for a moment, I have trouble catching my breath. But I won't fall apart. The way I'd behaved five years ago, and for too long after that, will never happen again. I'll take care of my sister this time. She won't be alone.

And somehow, some way, I will reunite with Jamie.

Once the car has moved out of sight, I walk into the house.

Calli sits there in a lump on the floor, just under the window, with her legs splayed and her head bowed, sobbing.

I kick the door shut and crouch in front of her. "Jesus, Calli. What can I do?"

She shakes her head while tears pour down her cheeks.

Yes, I *will* take care of my sister this time. So, I sit down beside Calli, tug her close to my side, and throw my arm around her. When I rest my chin on her head, she sags against me, her sobs growing louder and stronger, shaking her entire body.

"It'll be okay, Calli. One day it'll be okay, I promise."

"He's gone." Her voice had cracked on the final syllable. "I lost him."

"One thing I've learned about Aidan is that he's not the kind of guy who gives up easily. He loves you like crazy, and that's how I know he'll do whatever it takes to get back to you."

She buries her face against my chest and keeps on sobbing.

I've never seen my sister like this. Never. Not even when Mom and Dad died. I think she's broken right now because she held in all that grief for our parents and the strain of knowing she'd violated the law to help Rade. Losing Aidan was the last straw, and she can't hold it together anymore. But I'm here for her this time, and I won't leave until she's okay. Screw my job. Calli needs me.

We sit here sprawled on the floor while her sobs gradually become silent tears, and eventually, she stops crying altogether. Even when that happens, she doesn't move away from me and keeps her face buried against my chest. But she does unclench her hand, the one that had been fisted in my shirt. I switch from rocking her gently to just combing my fingers through her hair.

I get why Calli fell apart. She's never really had a boyfriend, much less been in love. I've watched her with Aidan, so I know what they have is real. Maybe even the fairy-tale kind of love.

Do Jamie and I have that? Not sure, but I want to find out.

At last, Calli raises her head. "Sorry I got your shirt all wet."

"It's just a little damp. Don't worry about it." I still have one arm around her, and she doesn't seem to mind that. "How do you feel? Sorry, that's a dumb question."

"No, it isn't. I feel like somebody shoved a melon baller inside my chest and scooped out my heart."

"I know. I felt that way when Leanne left me, though not because I wanted her back. I didn't love her the way you love Aidan."

She almost smiles. "But you love Jamie that way, don't you?"

"Yeah, I think I do."

"Then don't let her go. I want you to be happy, Gav. One of us should be, at least."

I kiss the top of her head. "Let's make you happy, then worry about me and Jamie."

We both get up and get on with life the best we can. I stick around until the next day, but then Calli insists I need to go home so I won't lose my job. She seems genuinely okay, in relative terms, and I believe it when she tells me she'll get through this ordeal.

Once I get back to my little apartment in Minneapolis, the first thing I do is call Jamie. We talk for an hour, but we both feel a little awkward about being happy while my sister and her brother are miserable. As the days go by, our phone calls become less awkward and more fun. We make each other laugh and talk about when we might get together again. Since Jamie has two rich brothers, and those guys share a private jet, it seems likely that she won't need to fly commercial to come visit me.

I want to go to Scotland right now. I need to pull her into my arms and kiss her until she's weak in the knees. When I tell Jamie I want to book a flight, she reminds me that Rory and Lachlan co-own a jet. Duh, I knew that. I guess I forgot because I feel weird about letting her brothers transport me to Scotland for free, but the longer I go without seeing her in person, the less I care about who pays for it.

Still, I can't leave America yet. Calli still has her divorce proceedings to worry about. I made a promise to myself that I would be here for my sister until her ordeal is over, and I won't renege on that. For the first two weeks after Aidan and Jamie went back to Scotland, I provide moral support for Calli while she deals with Rade and the divorce. At least the bastard relented at last, granting her a divorce and offering a financial settlement. In seven weeks, she will be free to marry Aidan.

"Don't jump the gun, Gav," my sister tells me as we're walking out of the lawyer's office. "Aidan and I still don't know if Seona's baby is his."

"But you love him like crazy, and I can't believe the universe would smack you both down like that."

She shrugs. "Life can really suck. Just have to pick yourself up and keep going, right?"

"Exactly."

Calli halts just as we're exiting the building. "You should go see Jamie. Or she should come to you."

"Uh, that statement came out of nowhere."

"No, it didn't. Make yourself happy, Gavin." She rubs her arms as if she's cold, though it's a warm day. "I just wish this divorce could be over today."

"Yeah, I know. My offer to beat the holy living shit out of Rade still stands. Just say the word."

"I appreciate that, but I don't think it will be necessary."

That afternoon, I fly home to Minneapolis—and I take my sister's advice. I make myself happy by calling Jamie. We talk for two hours. It's not enough, but it'll do for now. Jamie is happy to hear that Calli is almost free of her husband, but she also informs me of news at her end.

"Aidan is not the father of Seona's baby. We just heard the results of the paternity test. After that, Seona admitted that she'd slept with another man while she was with Aidan. At least that drama is over."

"That's great. I'm sure Calli and Aidan are relieved."

"Aye, they are." Jamie hesitates, and I swear I can almost hear her biting her lip. Maybe I just recognize the tone of her silence. Okay, that's dumb. But she does make a flat humming sound right before she speaks again. "You haven't heard, have you?"

"Heard what?"

"Aidan wants to marry Calli, but she threw him over."

"What?" I bolt upright. I'd been slouching in my easy chair, but Jamie's statement shocked me to my core. "Why the hell would Calli do that?"

"Dinnae know. She said goodbye to Aidan and hung up on him."

"Aw, shit. She's panicking." I slump into my chair again. "I need to call Tara. This is a two-person job."

"What is?"

"Talking my sister out of screwing up her life because she's afraid Aidan will turn into Rade."

"Good. That's exactly what I hoped you would say." She sighs. "Aidan is miserable, and I'm sure Calli is too."

Three days later, Tara and I knock on Calli's front door. She's stunned to see us, but happy too. We spend a good part of the day just hanging out with Calli until she finally fesses up and tells us everything. Aidan had written her the most romantic letter I've ever read, talking about how much he loves her and how much he needs her in his life. In the letter, Aidan told Calli to let me and Tara read it. He's a smart guy. Sharing his words with us finally helped my sister shake off her fears and realize what she needs to do.

"Jamie says Aidan is heartbroken," I tell my sister, "but he's trying to hide it. You're the same way, and if you don't get your ass on a plane right away, I'll hogtie you and send you to Aidan in a FedEx box."

Not sure if that threat is what pushed her in the right direction, but ten minutes later, Calli leaps off the sofa and stands up straighter than she has in weeks. "I'm going to Scotland to get my man."

Tara, the goofball, grins and squeals, leaping up and down. Then she hauls Calli into a bear hug that must be squeezing the life out of her. I can't help myself. Two of my favorite people in the world are happy, and I need to join in. It becomes a group hug. Then Calli rushes into the bedroom to pack her bags. Tara and I drive her to the airport, just to make sure she doesn't chicken out.

But I know she won't. Calli has shed her fears at last.

Now, if only I could do the same...

Eight weeks later, I'm flying to Scotland via MacTaggart Air—along with Tara and her husband, Blake. Calli and Aidan greet us at the Inverness airport, where we climb into a limo provided by Rory and Lachlan for the three-hour drive to the village where most of the MacTaggarts live. Two days later, I watch my baby sister marry a Scotsman in a cute little church on the outskirts of Loch Fairbairn, and later, we all travel to Lachlan and Erica's farm for the outdoor reception.

The weather gods blessed us with sunshine and warmth today. But I'd feel warm even if it were raining. This is the first time I've seen Jamie in person since she left Michigan.

We might have sneaked away to a secluded spot behind the barn to have a "wee poke," as Jamie calls it. We stay quiet enough that nobody will hear us, though some people might've noticed us skulking away. So what? I'm with the woman I love, the sky is blue, and Jamie feels incredible. When she comes, I seal my mouth over hers to mute her cries, right before I come too. Yeah, I'd stashed a box of condoms in my suitcase and slipped three of them into the inside pocket of my suit jacket.

It's been too damn long since I made love to this woman.

As the reception winds down, Aidan invites me to go into the house and have a "dram" of Scottish whisky with him in the kitchen. I can guess his real reason for the invite. So, it's no surprise when he finally speaks.

"Jamie is my sister and my best friend," he tells me, like I didn't already know that. "Dinnae break her heart, or I'll have to batter you bloody."

"I have no intention of breaking Jamie's heart. I love her, and I promise not to hurt her."

"Good. Now keep that vow."

Aidan loves his sister and would do anything for her. I can relate. If Aidan had kicked Calli to the curb, I would have pummeled him for sure. And I will do my best to show her family that I mean it when I say I never want to hurt her.

Chapter Twelve

Jamie

After the wedding, Gavin tells me he can only stay for two more days. He needs to get back to his job in Minneapolis. I understand that, but we barely have time to get reacquainted before he leaves, and the time we have left doesn't seem like enough. That's because it isn't enough. He still lives in America, and I still live here in Scotland. I never imagined I would become entangled in an intercontinental romance with an American man. My family has always assumed I would marry a good Scottish laddie.

Are they disappointed that I chose Gavin Douglas? Not entirely. He would fit right in with my cousins Magnus and Logan, if he gave them the chance. But Gavin didn't do much socializing at the wedding.

Now it's time for him to leave me.

We stand on the tarmac at the Inverness airport, holding hands, face to face, while we both struggle to figure out how to say goodbye. I'd been happy for several days because he was here. I dinnae want him to go.

"Take me with you," I say. "Please, Gavin, I'll miss you too much."

"Won't your family be pissed that I whisked you away without any warning?"

"Dinnae give a toss. Aidan ran away to America, so why shouldn't I? The last time I did that, no one minded."

He pulls me close, wrapping his arms around me. "I love you, Jamie, and nothing will change that. You don't need to jump on a plane with me to prove you feel the same way. I know it's true."

I rest my forehead on his chest, suddenly feeling deflated.

Gavin kisses the top of my head. "I'll come back as soon as I can, promise."

"But you've nearly used up your vacation days."

"I'll still have weekends off."

Lifting my head, I loop my arms around his neck. "Kiss me so thoroughly that I'll forget you're leaving until after the plane takes off."

He tugs me more firmly into his body, lowers his head, and—

My mobile pings, alerting me to a new text.

I shut my eyes and shake my head. *Mhac na galla.*

"Are you going to check that?"

"No. Ugh, yes." I dig the mobile out of my purse and check the new text. "It's Aidan. He says…run away to America with Gavin. We all agreed you should."

Gavin grabs my mobile and types on the screen, then hands the device back to me. "There. I made the decision for you, so you couldn't come up with reasons not to do it."

I should be very annoyed with him, but instead, I grin. "Let's get on the bloody plane before Lachlan realizes what he's done."

"Thought Aidan texted you."

"Aye, but Lachlan would have told him to do it."

Gavin steals my mobile again so he can dump it into my purse. Then he sweeps me up in his arms and carries me up the stairs and into the jet. I'd only ever flown in this jet twice, when I went to America on a trip that would change my life and when Aidan and I had to go home. Since I don't have a job right now anyway, I might as well go away with Gavin.

The co-pilot emerges from the cockpit and seems not the least confused that I'm on board. One of my brothers must have alerted the pilots. Once the co-pilot has shut the door, he disappears into the cockpit again.

Gavin takes my hand, leading me to a sofa, and we both sit down. "What was that thing you said when your phone pinged you?"

"What thing?" I suddenly realize what he's asking. "Oh, you mean the phrase I used. *Mhac na galla* means 'son of a bitch.' It's a Gaelic curse."

"I see. That's cool." He slings an arm across the sofa's back and leans in closer. "Got any dirty Gaelic phrases?"

"Oh, aye. Want to hear some?"

"Absolutely."

I lean toward him to whisper, "This jet has a bedroom."

"Let's go in there, so you can talk dirty Gaelic to me in private. That will probably wind up with us fucking."

I pretend to pout. "That would be just awful."

We retire to the bedroom and spend a good portion of the six-hour flight to Minneapolis in that room, shagging and laughing, while I teach Gavin all the dirty Gaelic words I know. By the time we reach our destination, he has become quite good at pronouncing Gaelic, and I love the phrases he has chosen to use. Rory had arranged for a limousine to pick us up at the airport and drive us to Gavin's wee apartment.

He winces as he opens the door and seems to be delaying, as if he worries I'll run back to Scotland once I see his home. But he finally swings the door open, and I walk inside.

Gavin shuts the door, leaning back against it while I explore the small space.

When I'm done, I face him. "Ahmno horrified, Gavin. You can relax. This is a cozy apartment. You even have a comfortable recliner."

"Yeah, but you're used to living in a castle."

I approach him, settling my hands on his chest. "I love you, Gavin. That means I would live in an igloo in the arctic to be with you."

He relaxes and almost smiles. "You're really not disgusted with my tiny, cramped, rundown hovel?"

"Not in the least." I take his hand, leading him over to the twin-size bed. "I'm sure we can both fit on this mattress. Let's make love."

He grins.

And we both undress. He insists on giving me plenty of foreplay, though I would've been fine with going straight to the shagging. I love that he wants to give me more than a quick poke. Gavin genuinely worries about my pleasure. And when he uses a bit of dirty Gaelic, I grow so aroused that I dinnae know how much longer I can wait to have him inside me.

He kneels over me, straddling my thighs, and skims his hand up and down his stiff cock. "Damn, Jamie, you are so beautiful. Need to push my *bigealais* inside your *baltan* and fuck you until I *caith*."

I know he will always make sure I come before he does. I don't need to hear him say the words. We make the wee bed creak in an erotic rhythm that matches our movements, and when we come at the same time, it feels like destiny.

Dinnae care how bloody stupid that sounds.

A few days later, I go home.

I'd love to say that in the following months our relationship remains rock solid and angst-free. But lying to myself won't help matters. Our long-distance romance comes with hiccups and false starts and a growing sense that we're drifting away from each other. I dinnae want that. Gavin doesn't either, I know. But we can't seem to find our way back to those easy, sweet days in Michigan when everything seemed perfect.

Gavin has to work overtime more often than either of us would like. That means I don't visit him in America more than once a month, and he begins to find excuses for why he can't come to Scotland. Gradually, once a month visits become once every other month, and I know something is wrong.

But Gavin won't talk to me.

In the meantime, my brother Rory returns from a business trip to New Orleans with a surprise. He married an American woman, Emery, and has brought her home to meet the family. We're all stunned beyond words. Rory has known Emery for barely more than four days. And he never told us he'd met anyone. Gavin and I fell in love quickly, but we haven't tied the knot. More than nine months has elapsed since those lovely days in Michigan, yet still, we're only dating—the intercontinental way.

At least we speak on the phone regularly, though those conversations have become somewhat strained.

When Rory comes home with his new wife, I don't have time to think about Gavin and our relationship. Since I've been living at Dùndubhan, I'm one of the first family members to meet Emery. She's bonnie and sweet, but also feisty enough to handle my brother. Rory seems a bit shell-shocked, and that means he gets grumpy. That doesn't faze Emery at all.

I instantly adore my newest sister-in-law. We hit it off like a house on fire.

Once we're all inside the castle, Rory finally introduces me. He seemed to have forgotten I existed. *Bod an Donais*, he must be completely in love with her to be so scatterbrained.

I seize Emery's arm. "Let me give you the tour. This house is really a castle, do ye know? Built in the Middle Ages."

"I knew it was a castle, yeah, but Rory hasn't been forthcoming with the details."

While Rory scowls at me, I shepherd Emery down the hall. "We'll start the tour here."

"Stop," my brother exclaims. "I will show my wife our home, if you please, Jamie."

"No need to shout at me. Ahmno deaf, Rory."

"Why don't you go to bed?"

I snort, thanks to the fact I'm trying not to laugh at him. "Ahmno five years old. It's only seven o'clock."

Mrs. Darroch, the housekeeper has been observing our exchange with definite amusement. She has always treated Rory like a son, which means she doesn't shy away from giving him a verbal spanking. But she doesn't need to do that now. Emery takes over that duty, and she does it expertly.

Aye, Rory has finally found his soul mate. We all know that—except for Rory.

The next day, we hold a family gathering in the garden at Dùndubhan to celebrate Rory's marriage. That's when I learn that my brothers have conspired to give me a surprise. A large, sexy surprise.

Gavin is here.

I race up to him and fling my arms around his neck, hugging him tightly. "I've missed you so much, *mo chridhe*."

"Missed you too, baby." He kisses me, crushing his mouth to mine despite my brothers watching us. "Feels so good to be with you again and hold you again."

We keep our arms around each other as we follow my brothers into the garden where so many MacTaggarts have gathered, from my immediate family to my cousins and uncles and aunts. Gavin and I get separated. The next time I see him, he's on the other side of the garden talking to Emery and seems uncomfortable being in a crowd of MacTaggarts.

Too soon, it's time for Gavin to leave. Watching him climb onto a jet and go home to America… That breaks my heart every time. I do get to see him again three weeks later for Rory and Emery's official wedding ceremony, the one my mother insisted they must have. We all know Sorcha MacTaggart gets her way. Even Rory, the Steely Solicitor, cannae say no to Ma.

Naturally, my brothers made sure to not only invite Gavin to the wedding, but to insist that he must come. So now, I wait on the tarmac to greet the man I love. The second he steps off the stairs,

I throw myself at him, showering him with kisses and hugs. He reciprocates in a similar manner, but after our initial reunion, we both seem to have trouble getting back into the groove, as Gavin would say. That night, we make love with a new intensity, as if we worry this will be the last time we see each other.

But now, Rory and Emery's wedding ceremony is about to begin.

Gavin and I sit beside each other, and I cry when Rory kisses Emery. But then, the crowd disperses and heads for the ceilidh in the great hall. I get one spin round the room with Gavin before the ceilidh becomes a merry-go-round of dancing with my relatives.

Then I notice that Emery's sister, Hadley, doesn't join in the dancing. She has her hands full with her twin girls. When I suggest to Gavin that we should help Hadley, he agrees. Now, Emery's sister can dance with her husband, Cole, while Gavin and I entertain the bairns. Gavin makes ridiculous faces and speaks in a silly voice to make them laugh, and he even shows them a magic trick. I had no idea he could do magic. I'm as enthralled by his antics as the bairns are.

When Lachlan and Aidan approach us, wearing grave expressions, I know something is wrong.

"Rory has gotten buckled," Lachlan explains. "That word is hardly adequate to describe his condition, since he's passed out, but that's not the point right now. We need to drag Rory upstairs. Gavin, could you please let Emery know what's happened?"

"Sure thing."

My brothers lead a wee parade with Gavin bringing up the rear, then he veers away to find Emery and give her the bad news. What in the world is wrong with Rory? I can't believe he would behave this way. Then again, he has been off kilter ever since he married Emery.

Gavin and I enjoy one more night in the castle. After that, he flies home to America. I am alone again. Aye, my family does their best to keep my spirits up in Gavin's absence, but they're more concerned for Rory—and they should be.

But I'm no longer privy to my brother's gnashing teeth and snarling. I decided it was best for Rory and Emery to have the castle to themselves while they sort out their relationship. For now, I'll be staying at Aidan and Calli's house where I can spend time with my wee niece. Emery says goodbye to me, but Rory is holed up in his office, and I agree with Emery when she suggests I shouldn't bother my brother right now.

Rory behaves rather badly for some time after the wedding, as if he's determined to chase Emery away. But she refuses to give up on him. He almost loses Emery because of his boorish behavior but finally realizes he made a huge mistake. He loves her deeply, a fact recognized by everyone except Rory. Emery, being a sweet and also practical woman, understands that his previous marriages damaged him. That's why he pushed her away. But Rory has declared his love for her at last, and she comes home to Dùndubhan, never to leave again.

If Rory could find his soul mate, why can't I? Gavin might be the one, and I have a newfound resolve to make our relationship work.

How will I do that? By whatever means necessary. Aye, that might be a vague plan, but I can flesh it out later. For tonight, I simply need to share my loosely conceived plan with my sister Fiona. She's very clever and more mature than I am, in terms of her age and her temperament.

"You want to do what?" Fiona says. "You're off your head, Jamie."

"Why? Rory married a woman after knowing her for four days. My idea is nowhere close to as barmy as that."

"Och, Jamie. What makes you think Gavin will agree to do it?"

"Because he loves me. But I need an excuse to ask him, and Ma and Da's anniversary is the perfect opportunity."

Fiona clucks her tongue. "Be careful. This might blow up in your face."

"A chance I will gladly take."

"If you insist, then…go for it."

This is an insane plan, for certain. But as the saying goes, desperate times call for desperate measures. Gavin and I have been apart too often lately, and I miss him terribly. This is the only option.

I'm going to get my man.

Chapter Thirteen

Gavin

I'm sitting in my tiny apartment on a Friday night, wiped out from work and ready to hit the hay, half asleep already. Then someone rings my doorbell. I never realized that thing even worked. Nobody rings the bell. They just bang on the door instead. It's a sad commentary on the modern world when ringing a doorbell becomes too onerous a task for anyone to bother with. But who the heck is knocking at this hour? It's almost ten o'clock.

Yawning, I hoist my sorry ass out of my recliner and shuffle to the door. I pull it open without even thinking to look through the peephole.

Jamie grins at me. "Surprise!"

"What?" I gape at her, not sure if I'm awake or asleep. Then I feel drool on the corner of my mouth and realize this can't be a dream. I hastily wipe the saliva off with the hem of my T-shirt. "Jamie? I thought you couldn't make it here for another two weeks."

"I couldn't wait any longer. I miss you."

She leaps into my arms, trusting me to catch her. I do, of course, but I'm still kind of confused. For a moment, though, I just hold her and relish the warmth and softness of her body pressed to mine. It's been too damn long since we saw each other in person.

Finally, I set her down on her feet. "I've missed you too, Jamie. But why didn't you let me know you were coming? I would've picked you up at the airport."

"I wanted to surprise you." She gives me an impish smile. "Cannae do that if you know in advance."

"Uh, yeah, I get that."

She leans sideways to peer past my shoulder. "May I come in? Or do you have another girlfriend hiding in there?"

"Yeah, I'd better tell my three other girlfriends to skedaddle." I pick her up and carry her into the tin-can apartment, setting her down on the recliner. "Are you hungry? No, you probably ate on the plane. I mean, it comes with a gourmet chef, for pity's sake."

Jamie studies me for a moment. "Are you jealous that Rory and Lachlan lent me their jet to get me here?"

"No. Well, maybe." I drop onto the bed, which places me less than five feet away from her. "I'm tired, Jamie. I had a long week at work."

"Let's go to sleep, then. We can talk in the morning."

She jumps out of her chair and insists on pulling the covers back for me. Then the woman I adore casually strips and climbs onto the bed. I struggle to get undressed. My exhaustion makes it a lot more difficult, but eventually, I'm naked. So, I crawl onto the bed to lie down beside her.

I must've fallen asleep instantly, because the next thing I know, it's morning and I'm alone in bed. For a few seconds, I think Jamie must have snuck out in the middle of the night and gone back to Scotland. But then I hear sizzling sounds coming from the kitchen. I haven't opened my eyes yet. Jamie is humming a melodic tune, and I just lie here for a while listening to her. After a few minutes, her humming turns into singing as she softly croons a pretty tune that I know I've heard before, though I can't remember the name of it. Probably something Scottish. Jamie loves the traditional songs.

But I've never heard her sing before. She has a beautiful voice.

I drag my butt out of bed and get dressed. Jamie smiles when she realizes I'm up and awake, but she doesn't stop singing. Good. I want to hear more of her voice. I walk up to the kitchen island, which is more like an islet considering the mini size of everything in this apartment. There's only one stool at the island, but I pull that up to the counter and rest my arms on it, enjoying the serenade from a hot Scottish lass.

Jamie raises onto her tiptoes to lean across the islet and kiss me. "*Madainn mhath*, Gavin. That means good morning."

"Good morning to you too, Jamie. Are you starting me on a Gaelic language course?"

"Not officially. But I would love to teach you, if you're interested."

"Sure, sounds like fun. The only language I really know is English—the American version. I took Spanish in high school, since it was required, but I don't remember any of it these days."

Jamie slants across the counter to kiss me again. "Once I teach you Gaelic, you'll never forget it."

"I'm sure you're right. By the way, what was that song you were singing?"

"The Elfin Knight."

"Are you serious? Scots have a song about an elf who's a knight too? That doesn't sound like anything your brothers would sing about. Can't picture Lachlan riding an elf horse. He'd break its little back."

Jamie raises a spatula, aiming it at me. "Dinnae be sarcastic about a traditional folk song. Scots love The Elfin Knight. It's about a lass who is sitting on a hill when she hears the blare of an elf knight's horn and wishes he would come to her bedroom."

"A spicy Scottish folk song? I'm starting to like this. Tell me the rest."

"Dinnae remember the whole story. But I do recall that the elfin knight shows up in her bed chamber and makes some sort of deal with her that results in the lass marrying the knight. She performs tasks for him, though I can't remember the details offhand."

"So, he blows his horn to attract a girl, then screws her and gets her to do stuff for him. Do they live happily ever after?"

Jamie shrugs. "I reckon so."

"Damn, Scots are so weird."

"In the oldest version of the ballad, the lass has no choice in the matter. The elfin knight plans to defile her without her consent. I prefer the later version because the lass isn't a victim in that story."

"Yeah, I wouldn't like the older version either."

Jamie sets two plates on the island. "Let's eat."

I jump off the stool as she comes around to my side. Though she tries to push me back onto the stool, I'm bigger and can easily overwhelm her. I don't need to do that, however. She relents and sets her sexy little ass on the stool. I jump up to sit on the countertop.

We talk about that song some more, making jokes about it and generally enjoying ourselves. I hadn't realized how lonely I was until Jamie turned up last night. We talk on the phone a lot, but that's not the same thing as being together in person, in the same place. I've missed the hell out of her. Not sure how much longer I can stand to be away from her, but I can't ask Jamie to move to America for me. The MacTaggarts are all very close, especially Jamie and her brothers and sisters. Now that my sister lives in Scotland too, maybe I should move there.

To another country? Where the people speak so differently? I feel anxious just thinking about that.

Sure, I know Scots basically speak the same language as Brits and Americans. But they have strange slang, and there's the whole Gaelic issue. Jamie taught me some dirty Gaelic, but that won't help me in everyday life. I meant it when I said I'd love to learn the language. I'd probably suck at it, though. Despite learning Spanish in high school, the only phrase I remember is "*buenos dias.*" I think that means "good morning."

If I can't assimilate with the MacTaggarts…will Jamie dump me?

The lass in question raises one hand to touch my cheek. "What's fashing you, Gavin?"

Another Scottish word—"fash." I know that asking what's fashing me means she wants to know what's wrong, but hearing that term only brought home the reality of the language difference. Am I being a dick and a dope? Should I fall to one knee and beg her to marry me, damn the consequences? That's what I've wanted to do since the day we met.

"Well, Gav? What's fashing you? I'm asking—"

"I know what you're asking. What's bothering me is that when I think about us, I flash back to the day I met Aidan. He wasn't thrilled to find out that I was attracted to his sister." I down a mouthful of coffee a little too fast, making me cough. Jamie sits there serenely waiting for me to speak again. "I'm starting to feel like I'm the elfin knight who's trying to whisk you away from your family so I can do naughty things to you."

"Dinnae think the song mentions the lass's family."

"Yeah, but the knight was an outsider."

Jamie slides off the stool and wraps her arms around me. She presses her cheek to my belly, since she can't reach my chest when I'm sitting on the counter. "You *are* my knight, Gav. You swept me off my feet and made me feel like a maiden in one of those medieval romances."

I brush my fingers through her hair while she gazes up at me with the sweetest look on her face. "I don't want to disappoint you,

Jamie. Not sure your brothers will ever really accept me, not to mention all your cousins who probably want to murder me. Logan for sure would want that."

"He was a spy, but he's a sweet man at heart."

"If you say so. He gives me the 'I could kill you with one finger' look every time I see him."

Jamie lifts her head and pulls it back a touch. "Do you feel inadequate because the men in my extended family are tough?"

"Inadequate? No, I don't think so." Do I feel that way? Never really thought about it until Jamie mentioned the possibility. "Well, I don't know. Maybe I sort of, kind of feel that way."

She backs away, waving for me to jump off the island. Once I hop down, she grabs my hand. "Let's do something fun today. Something that will make you feel reinvigorated and full of machismo."

A laugh splutters out of me. "Machismo? Come on, Jamie, I'm not that much of a wuss. Am I?"

"Of course not. But I think you need to do something other than answering phone calls all day. Something that will remind you of what a virile, powerful, sexy, braw man you are."

The way her voice dropped to a lower key when she called me virile and all that other stuff… It makes me feel like a man again. Not that I ever felt like I wasn't a man. Jeez, even in my head I sound wimpy. Time to fix that issue.

I pull Jamie into my body. "Let's get wild together—in and out of bed."

We get on my computer and search for exciting things we can do together—outdoors. I decided we've done enough hanging out inside my apartment, and it's time to have an open-air adventure. Jamie agreed. Actually, she grinned, jumped up and down, and high-fived me three times. She also slapped my ass, but I slapped hers right back. Jamie calls it my "erse," though. It's the Scottish word for her cute little caboose.

Jamie laughs. "What did you just call my erse, Gav?"

"Your caboose. I could've used a variety of other terms for your cute ass. Booty, heinie, keister, patootie—"

"Puh-what-ee?" she says with a half-suppressed laugh.

"Patootie. It's an American thing."

"I see." She grabs my ass. "Whatever you call it, your erse is mine."

Yeah, I feel better already. There's nothing like teasing Jamie to make me feel good again.

Since it's a beautiful, warm late summer's day, we agree to go skydiving as our first adventure in what will become a two-day experience. Neither of us has ever done anything like this before. My job in the Marines had been ground-based. I was never a paratrooper. But maybe what I've really needed ever since I came back from Afghanistan was to jump out of my comfort zone—literally.

There's nobody I'd rather do that with than Jamie.

After receiving some training, we get to skydive tandem. I take the reins while Jamie just hangs on for the ride, strapped to my body. The minutes fly by thanks to the adrenaline boost brought on by sheer excitement, and I'm sure Jamie feels the same way. Then it's time for us to fly. We leap out of the plane, soaring through the sky, sailing down, down, down. I pull our chutes just like the instructor told us, and our descent slows but still gives us plenty of time to appreciate our view of the earth from high above. Then we touch down in the grassy field next to the airstrip.

Once we've ditched our chute, Jamie leaps on me with her arms and legs wrapped around me. Then she throws her head back and whoops.

I chuckle. "Guess you liked that, huh?"

"No, I bloody loved it!"

"Me too. But now we have a decision to make."

She slides down my body slowly until her feet hit the ground. "What should we do next. That's the decision."

"Exactly."

We return to my car and browse options on my cell phone, searching for something that's less of an adrenaline rush after our skydiving fun. We finally choose kayaking. A lot of places not far from Minneapolis offer those kinds of experiences, and the best part is that we won't require any training. We'll be able to just hop in a kayak and go. The company we select gives us a map with their recommended route, which will give us the chance to see lots of wildlife, including birds.

Jamie loves that. She's an outdoorsy girl. One of the first things I learned about her once we seriously started dating was that she loves bicycling through the villages of Loch Fairbairn and Ballachulish. I haven't had the chance to do that with her yet, but I'd love to.

I would go anywhere with this woman.

Chapter Fourteen

Jamie

Oh, I love kayaking with Gavin while surrounded by the most beautiful scenery I've ever seen in America. To be fair, I haven't seen much of this country. I wish I had suggested we do this months ago. Gavin has relaxed and become the man I knew when we first met—strong, clever, full of humor, and ready for anything that I want to try. Flying to America to see him had been the best thing I could've done for our floundering relationship. My surprise arrival had reawakened Gavin—and me too.

We're kayaking along the Chain of Lakes which, as the name implies, consists of three interconnected bodies of water. We visit all of them—Lake of the Isles, Lake Calhoun, and Lake Harriet—while enjoying the scenery and the wildlife. We see multiple species of geese as well as ducks and swans, not to mention land-based birds like partridges, pheasants, hawks, doves, and even eagles.

I just stop myself from shrieking when I see my first bald eagle. Dinnae want to scare it away. We don't have those birds in Scotland, and I love getting such a close-up view of America's most famous eagle species. Gavin even manages to take a picture of the bald eagle so I'll have a memento of our adventure today.

But I don't need a photograph to remember this day.

After enjoying a delicious lunch at a restaurant, we go on a self-guided walking tour of sights along the Mississippi River. I never knew just how wide the river is until I saw it in person. Pictures and films don't do it justice. Gavin suggests we should walk across the Stone Arch Bridge so I can get a better view of St. Anthony Falls. It's impressive, to say the least. The bridge used to be for trains only. Gavin tells me about that, and I try to pay attention to everything he says, but I keep getting distracted by the scenery.

My day with Gavin has been the best time we've ever had together.

The man I adore wants to take me to a posh hotel for the night, but I assure him he doesn't need to do that. I'm happy to stay at his apartment. But I soon realize that he suggested a hotel because he wants that, though he won't tell me that straight out. So, I relent and allow him to spoil me. If it makes him happy, which it clearly does, then it makes me happy too.

But now it's time for me to go home.

Gavin drives me to the airport, but I don't need to go through security. Having brothers who co-own a private jet has its perks, that's for dead sure. Gavin walks with me across the tarmac and even climbs onto the jet with me. Then he pulls me close and simply cradles my head to his chest as if he doesn't want to let me go. I feel that way about him too. The longer our relationship stays intercontinental, the more I feel as if we will never be able to get married and live in the same house, much less in the same country.

"I've got some vacation time left," Gavin tells me. "I could see if I can take four or five days off to go to Scotland."

My head pops up. "You want to do that?"

"Yeah. I mean, it's not like I've never gone there before. But it would be great to have more than two days with you."

"I would love that."

"Then it's settled. I'll find out how soon I can use those vacation days."

"Oh, Gav, thank you." I pepper kisses all over his face. "I love you so much."

Though I would never tell him so, all this traveling back and forth between America and Scotland has become exhausting. Now that Calli has married Aidan, and they live in the Highlands, I cannae see what's preventing Gavin from moving there too. His cousin Tara is married, so he wouldn't be abandoning her. Besides, he's lived away from Tara for a long time. Why won't Gavin even talk about the prospect of moving to Scotland? I know he'd love it there if he stopped worrying about everything.

We have occasionally discussed the possibility of one of us moving so we could be together. But the pain and guilt he still feels, about his parents and the way he abandoned Calli after their death, keeps him rooted in place. I know his military experience left him battered emotionally and physically. But he can't hold on to all that pain forever. Can he?

"We're about to take off," the co-pilot says. He's standing near the doorway, waiting for Gavin to leave.

I kiss him and smile. "Go on. We'll see each other soon."

He stares at me for a moment, then crushes me to his body, kissing me with such passionate desperation that I almost want to cry. Then he touches his head to mine and jogs down the stairs.

I watch out the window as Gavin keeps jogging away from the plane. He pauses only long enough to wave at me before he disappears from view.

Six hours later, I'm back in Scotland. Alone.

Well, all right, I'm not actually alone. I have my extended family to keep me company. I've been staying with Aidan and Calli ever since Rory married Emery, so I expect one or both of them to greet me when I walk out of the jet. But instead, Rory and Lachlan are there.

"What's wrong?" I ask as I approach them. "You look like you have bad news. Did Erica and Emery both boot you out of your homes?"

Rory rolls his eyes. "There is no bad news. And no, our wives have not booted us out of anywhere."

"Then why are you and Lachie here?"

Peripherally, I can see Lachlan grimacing—because I used his diminutive. But he doesn't speak up to complain.

"We've all agreed," Rory says, "that you shouldn't continue living with Aidan and Calli. You were never meant to be their permanent nanny."

"But I love spending time with the bairn."

"Aye. But we've decided you should go elsewhere."

"Such as where? The moon?"

Lachlan shakes his head. "No, ye cheeky lass. We want you to move in with Fiona and Cat."

"Oh, I see. Thank you for the offer, but I'd rather not stay with them. Fiona and Cat might feel slighted because I have a boyfriend and they don't."

"They dinnae care, I'm sure. What's the real reason you'd rather not stay with your sisters?"

"My boyfriend might be coming to visit, and I dinnae think Fiona or Cat wants to hear me and Gav shagging."

"*Bod an Donais*," Rory says miserably. "How many times have we asked you lasses not to bring up the subject of your love lives in front of us?"

"At least a hundred times."

Lachie and Rory whisper to each other for a moment, then Rory faces me. "You will be a guest at Dùndubhan for the time being."

"Thank you, Rory."

"What about me?" Lachlan says. "It was a joint decision."

"Aye, also thank you, Lachie. My brothers are so generous in the way they order their sisters about."

He squints at me, but Lachlan knows that won't fash me. Rory knows it too, but at least he has the sense not to let his displeasure show on his face.

I'd lived at Dùndubhan for nearly a year before Rory married Emery, so it's like coming home when I arrive at the castle again. Lachlan drives back to Ballachulish, to the farm he and Erica own just outside the village, while Rory and I head for Dùndubhan. The moment we enter the vestibule, Emery and Mrs. Darroch suddenly appear from the vicinity of the kitchen to greet us. Mrs. Darroch hugs me and kisses my cheek. But Emery is far more boisterous in her greeting.

She seizes me in a hug so firm that I gasp. "Oh, Jamie, we're so happy to have you at Dùndubhan again. And Lachlan called to tell us that Gavin might be coming for an extended visit. That's wonderful!"

"Aye, it is. Cannae wait to see him again, even though I just spent the weekend with him in Minneapolis."

"Being away from your honey is awful. When Rory went to Paris for a few days to attend a conference, I missed him like crazy." She aims a sly glance at her husband. "Of course, Rory was only trying to hide from me. The conference was a ruse."

Rory rolls his eyes, as he often does. "Em, dinnae tell lies to Jamie. It wasn't completely a ruse. I did learn new things at the conference."

"Uh-huh." She winks at him. "You learned how to avoid your wife."

"But I will never do that again. You are my soul mate, *mo chridhe*."

Rory MacTaggart just used the phrase soul mate. I cannae believe it. Though I know Emery has changed my brother's life and his attitudes toward everything, I hadn't expected him to announce that out loud.

If Lachlan and Rory could change… Maybe Gavin and I have a chance too.

Ten days later, I'm once again standing on the tarmac at the Inverness airport waiting for one of the pilots to open the jet's door. The moment Gavin steps out of the jet and onto the stairs, I rush toward the bottom of the steps. He jogs down them and pulls me into his arms, kissing me so thoroughly that I feel soft and warm and melty. Aye, Emery taught me the word melty. My newest sister-in-law is my favorite person in the world—after Gavin. No one will ever displace him in my heart.

He finally peels his lips away from mine. "So damn glad to see you, baby."

My heart swells at those simple words. "I couldn't sleep last night because I was so excited to see you again."

"Can we go straight to your bedroom and make love?"

I bite my lip and lift my brows. "We could do that in the car. Rory sent me here in a limousine that I know for a fact has a privacy partition."

He chuckles. "I love how hot you always are for me. That's a great idea. I've never done it in any kind of vehicle."

"Does a private jet count as a vehicle?"

"No, it's an airplane." He grasps my erse. "So, this will be a first for us."

"Brilliant! Take me to the limousine—and *in* the limousine, please."

He salutes. "Yes, ma'am."

Then he picks me up and carries me over to the waiting vehicle. The driver doesn't even bat an eye when Gavin asks for the privacy partition to be lowered. I reckon the driver has done that many times for clients who do business in the car, and perhaps even for randy lovers like me and Gavin.

We have three and a half hours to enjoy each other in this car.

Gavin slides a hand up my thigh, and even through my jeans, I swear I can feel the heat of his skin. "Wanna get naked? Or mess around with our clothes on?"

"I've never 'messed around' while fully clothed. So do whatever you want, Gav. I need you to fuck me, that's all."

"You are the best girl any man could hope to find."

He slides that hand up to my waistband. When he unhooks the button on my jeans, my breath catches. But when he pulls the zipper down slowly, my pulse accelerates and my skin grows sensitive, so much that the slightest touch drives me mad with desire for him.

Gavin pushes his hand inside my knickers, cupping me there. "Fuck, you're already wet for me. I can smell it and feel it all over my palm."

"Oh, God, I love the way this feels. Dinnae stop, Gav, please."

"I'm going to take it so slow that you'll be panting for me."

He gently separates my folds and glides one finger down to pet my clitoris. His fingers move so slowly and delicately that the sensation drives me mad, and I begin to thrust my hips without any conscious decision to do that. My body has a mind of its own. No, that's not true. Gavin commands my body, and I love letting him take control of me.

I slap my hands down on his thighs and grip them so tightly that he sucks in a sharp breath. Then my hands drift up to his hips. While he spreads his fingers to rub my folds, using only his thumb to torment my nub, I cannae stop myself from rubbing his cock through his jeans.

He's breathing as hard as I am. "Fuck, Jamie, don't do that unless you want me to come in my pants. I'd rather come inside you."

I peel my hand away. "Sorry. Couldn't help myself."

Gavin latches his mouth on to my breast, suckling it through my blouse. The fabric isn't enough of a barrier. While he goes on sucking my nipple, I grow so painfully aroused that I begin to pant and moan. Instead of gripping his cock, I clench the edge of the seat and squeeze my eyes shut, just waiting for the moment when he will push me over the edge.

"Come for me, baby, come for me now."

I throw my head back, my mouth open on a strangled cry—and I come. My muscles clench nothing, until he shoves two fingers inside me. He pumps them in and out, powerfully and swiftly, while he keeps suckling my nipple. That sends a pulse of pleasure barreling down my nerves, intensifying my orgasm.

He releases my nipple and seals his mouth over mine, swallowing my cries.

When it's over, I sag against the seat. My breaths come hard and fast, just like my heartbeats.

Someone knocks on the partition.

"*Mhac na galla*," I hiss. "What the bloody hell is that?"

Gavin seems dazed as he stares at the partition.

"Sorry to bother you," the driver shouts through the barrier. "Just got news."

News? What? Dinnae understand the word. An incredible climax delivered by an incredible man will do that to a lass.

Gavin shakes off his confusion before I do. He shouts to the driver, "Just a minute." Then he turns to me. "Zip up, Jamie."

"Huh?" I blink rapidly and at last manage to clear my head. I zip up my jeans and shout to the driver, "You can lower the partition."

The barrier rolls down, revealing the driver's face inch by inch. His expression is a wee bit pinched. "I apologize for the interruption. Just got a text from your brother Rory. We're picking up another passenger."

"Passenger?" I glance at Gavin, but he simply shrugs. "Do you know who it is?"

"Aye. It's Evan MacTaggart."

"Oh. Well, thank you for letting us know."

"Should I raise the partition?"

"No, that won't be necessary." Because we won't be shagging in this car today.

Chapter Fifteen

Gavin

I can't believe this. Though I love giving Jamie orgasms, the driver's announcement has left me in a bad way. I'm so hard that I think my jeans might split open. Watching Jamie come always affects me that way. Still, I'm glad I could give her pleasure, even if I didn't get any myself. A gentleman always makes sure a lady has everything she wants and needs, no matter what.

Ten minutes later, when we reach an apartment building on the other side of Inverness, my stiff problem has softened considerably. Thank goodness. Jamie's cousin Evan has just climbed into the limo.

He sits down on the bench seat that faces us and smiles at Jamie. "It's good to see you, *gràidh*. Sorry we haven't seen each other more often, but my work has consumed me lately."

"No worries, Evan. We're all so proud of your accomplishments."

The guy seems a touch uncomfortable with Jamie's praise. But he shakes it off and looks at me. "You must be the American laddie who has stolen my cousin's heart."

I hold out my hand to him. "Gavin Douglas. Your cousin Aidan is married to my sister."

Evan shakes my hand. "Pleasure to meet you. I met Calli briefly at the wedding ceilidh for Rory and his new bride. Your sister is a lovely lass."

The three of us have a nice conversation for the first hour of our journey, but then Evan tells us he needs to do some work on his computer. He's some kind of tech genius, according to Jamie. I talk my "lass" into playing gin rummy with me to pass the time. Evan smirks at that suggestion, which I assume means he doesn't think we can play a card game on the backseat of a limo. But we have no trouble playing the game this way. Jamie and I sit sideways on the seat, facing each other, and we both sit cross-legged too.

So much for the tech genius knowing everything.

Maybe I do rib Evan a little bit, but he clearly doesn't mind. In fact, about two hours and fifteen minutes into our journey, he asks if he can get in on the gin rummy action. We play a three-way game with Evan sitting on the floor with his cards on the seat between me and Jamie. I'd kind of assumed Evan was an uptight geek, but he's actually pretty cool. Not the laugh-riot type of guy. But he can relax enough to enjoy a card game and even make a few jokes.

Jamie loves all of it. Every time she wins a hand, she throws her arms up and cheers—though she keeps her cries muted enough that the driver won't crash the car. Jamie has perfected the shrieking version of golf claps. It's the cutest thing ever.

We drop Evan off at his mom's house, then continue on to Dùndubhan. We both wind up taking a joint nap with my arm around her shoulders and her head on my chest, waking up only once we reach the castle. The driver gently rouses us. As we climb out of the limo, Rory and Emery emerge from the vestibule to greet us.

Jamie hugs them both. I hug Emery but shake Rory's hand. Guys like us don't do the hugging thing with each other.

Before we walk into the castle, I take a moment to enjoy the sunset. With my arm around Jamie, we both gaze up at the golden rays as they sink toward the horizon and streamers of deep pink and orange fill the sky. I've never been the type to study a sunset, but being with Jamie has turned me into a sentimental fool—and I don't care.

Mrs. Darroch has gone home, which means she walked across the courtyard to the little cottage alongside the walled garden. But she left us a great snack. The four of us enjoy the food the housekeeper made, but we don't talk about the elephant in the kitchen. That would be me and my relationship with Jamie. Our weekend in Minneapolis had been incredible, but now we're back in MacTaggart territory.

And I'm the invader.

Rory and Emery head up to the top floor, where they have a huge bedroom. Jamie and I will stay on the ground floor, in one of the bedrooms in the guest wing. That means we can make all the noise we want.

Tonight, though, we're too tired for sex.

In the morning, it's raining. No golden sunrise to match yesterday's golden sunset. Oh, well. I've got the human version of a stunning sunrise lying beside me in this bed. I wake up with Jamie snuggled against me. We're facing each other, so I can just lie here watching her while she sleeps and count the smattering of faint freckles on her cheeks.

She sighs and stretches, keeping her eyes shut.

I brush a lock of hair away from her face. "Good morning, baby."

Jamie slowly peels her lids open and gives me a sleepy-sexy smile. "Good morning, Gavin."

"What amazing adventures would you like to have today?"

"Let's go into Loch Fairbairn and visit Kirsty's shop."

"That would be the metaphysical shop, right? And Kirsty is one of your cousins."

"Aye. She has two sisters, Isla and Elspeth, as well as a brother, Logan."

"Yeah, I've met him. Not the sisters, though." I sit up and pat her bottom. "Time to get off your patootie and get dressed."

She laughs. "Had you ever actually used the word patootie before that morning in your apartment?"

"No. But I've decided it describes your ass perfectly."

"Hmm." She rolls onto her back and stretches languorously. "What should I call your erse? 'Caboose' is intriguing, but I think 'booty' suits you best."

"Scots don't have any words other than 'erse' to describe someone's heinie?"

"That's the only one I've ever used."

A fist raps on the bedroom door. "Rise and shine, Jamie and the American *cacan*. Breakfast will be served in the dining room in precisely eighteen minutes."

Oh, yeah, even if Rory wasn't the only other man in the castle this morning, I'd still know that was him. He's teasing me with the "*cacan*" thing. I know that word means "wee shit." I've been dating his sister, after all, and sweet Jamie loves to curse in Gaelic. Despite the way her brothers behave, I don't believe they want to chase me away. Why would Rory let me stay in his castle if he wanted me gone? No, I think he and his brothers just want to harass me to make sure I won't break Jamie's heart.

I never want to do that. And I admire her brothers for their commitment to protecting Jamie without directly interfering in our relationship. I have a sister too, and I would do anything I could to prevent Calli from getting hurt. Luckily, she married Aidan, a nice guy who I know would never hurt my sister.

Jamie and I get up and get dressed, then head for the dining room. It's just at the end of the guest-wing hallway, so we don't have far to walk. When we traipse into the dining room, Rory and Emery are already seated and waiting for us. Rory sits at the head of the table, naturally, with Emery at his right.

I pull out a chair for Jamie, and as she sits down, she smiles up at me.

Rory gives me an appreciative nod. Did I just gain a small measure of approval from the Steely Solicitor? I think maybe I did.

Jamie is sitting directly across from Emery, right next to Rory. I take the chair beside hers, and Emery winks at me. No idea what that means. Emery is very smart and kind, but she's also sorta weird. I guess it takes an unusual woman to tame a man like Rory.

We all have a nice conversation over breakfast, discussing mundane things—until Emery brings up Halloween.

She sets her arms on the table and smiles with a touch of mischief. "We need to throw a big Halloween party here at Dùndubhan."

Rory rolls his eyes. "Why, Em, do we need that?"

"For fun. You finally unleashed your wild side, and I'd bet you have never attended any kind of party, much less a costume bash."

"Aye, and there's a bloody good reason for that." He leans forward slightly and squints at his wife. "Because I despise parties."

"Oh, come on, Rory Baby. Let's have a big bash."

He squints harder. "I've repeatedly asked you never to call me that in front of other people."

Emery tries to suppress a laugh, but she winds up spluttering instead. "Everyone already knows I call you Rory Baby. The cat's out of that bag and scurrying around the house, scratching up all your precious furniture. Get over it, sweetie."

Damn, I love Emery more every time I see her. She's awesome.

I might be smirking now. Can't help it. Watching a blonde bombshell basically tell her much-larger husband to lighten up and grow a pair is one of the highlights of my life so far.

Rory relaxes and smiles, grasping his wife's hand so he can kiss it. "You're right, *mo gaoloch*. A Halloween ceilidh would give us an excuse to bring the entire clan together. I cannot promise I will enjoy every moment of it, but I will give it a go."

Emery grins and claps three times. "Yay! Thank you, Rory Baby. You're the sweetest."

He smiles with a touch of bemusement and relaxes in his chair.

Will Jamie and I ever have the kind of relationship these two have? Well, I can't really compare our relationships. Rory married Emery four days after they met in New Orleans. Jamie and I have been navigating an intercontinental romance for more than a year.

After breakfast, Jamie and I go for a walk. There's a trail on the far side of the castle that leads to the river. It's nice to spend some time outdoors with the lass I love, rather than just hanging out inside. Our weekend trips to see each other don't give us much of a chance to relax. We both feel compelled to find activities to do together, to make the most of our brief in-person visits.

Strolling with Jamie makes me feel like all that stress has vanished.

We sit down on the banks of the river, which Jamie tells me has no name. That's weird, but I'd rather focus on her than on finding out why Rory's river has no name. We have our arms around each other's waists as we amble long, listening to birdsongs and the rushing of the water. I can't help imagining us walking like this with our children. In my fantasy, we have two kids, a boy and a girl, but that brings up a question in my mind. If we have kids, will they speak with Scottish accents or American ones?

Don't care. I'll love them either way.

But will they be raised in Scotland? Will I need to get dual citizenship?

Jamie rubs her cheek on my arm. "What are you thinking about, Gavin? You seem very serious."

"No, it's nothing. Just lost in my own thoughts." I kiss the top of her head. "Maybe we should come up with potential names for the river, just for the heck of it."

Didn't I deftly change the subject? I don't want to explain my weird, silly thoughts to her, not yet. If we get engaged, maybe I will tell her.

"Are you sure everything is all right?" Jamie asks. "You know you can tell me anything."

"I swear it's nothing, honestly." Yeah, that didn't sound guilty at all. "Don't you like my idea that we should invent names for the river?"

"Aye, I do like that. It sounds like something Rory would positively hate, so we should definitely do it." She bumps into me on purpose, gazing up at me with the sweetest impish smile. "It would be fun to watch Rory's face turn bright red."

I chuckle. "You're a naughty lass, aren't you?"

"Aye. But you love that about me."

"Yep, always have, always will."

But more than that, I will love this woman forever. Unless she dumps me first. I don't mention that thought to Jamie. It's dumb and nothing but a passing worry.

We spend the remainder of my vacation days however Jamie wants. She insists I should tell her what I'd like to do, but I prefer to let her act as my tour guide to the Highlands. After all, this is her home. I love the way she lights up when she points out her favorite places on a map, so she can devise the best itinerary for our day trips. Every evening, we go back to Dùndubhan to have dinner with Rory and Emery—and whoever else might show up. Jamie's relatives have a way of just appearing suddenly in the dining room doorway. It's kind of weird, but I've gotten used to it.

Mostly, it's her immediate family who magically appear. But I have met a few of her cousins, of which there a shocking number around these parts.

"Oh, aye," she agrees when I share my thoughts with her. "There are MacTaggarts everywhere. We're a wee bit like ants. We emerge from under a rock to crawl about and overtake you when we're least expected. Sort of like the blob in that old science fiction film."

"Your metaphors are weird and kind of sinister, but I think that's cute."

She kisses my cheek. That's what Jamie does whenever I say something that she labels "barmy," but she's even cuter when she informs me that I might be "off my head" if I think danger is adorable.

But soon, it's time for me to fly home. I do have a job, after all, though I'd much rather stay here with Jamie. She offers to go home with me, though I assure her that's unnecessary. We can talk on the phone, after all, or even do video calls. After six days with Jamie in Scotland, I feel refreshed and ready to go.

Everything gets back to normal, but not for long.

Six weeks after I came back from the Highlands, my boss calls me into his office. I can tell by the look on his face that he isn't about to give me a promotion or a raise. By the time he stops babbling meaningless boss-talk, I've already guessed what he wants to tell me. All that's left is for him to say the words.

"I'm sorry, Gavin. I have to let you go."

"Yeah, I figured."

"The company has been going through a rough time, financially, and we need to cut the wheat from the chaff." He hands me an actual pink slip and actually expects me to take it. "I truly am sorry. You've been a dedicated employee, but your sales volume was lower than that of other associates."

Since he's still thrusting that pink piece of paper at me, I give up and take it.

My former boss looks obviously relieved, like he expected me to karate kick him in the nuts. "Please gather your personal items and relinquish your badge at the security station downstairs."

"Uh-huh."

I trudge out of his office and collect up the few items on my desk that belong to me. Then I trudge downstairs to hand my employee badge to a stern pseudo-cop who analyzes it for several seconds before he tells me I can leave.

Yeah, my life is so amazing. How can I tell Jamie I'm an unemployed loser? She doesn't have a job either, but I would never ask her to support me while I hunt for another crappy position. What am I qualified for? Ground ordnance maintenance isn't a popular search on job sites. It's a military thing. And my years of working for Rapid React didn't qualify me for anything other than annoying innocent people with cold calls.

Tomorrow, I'm supposed to fly to Scotland for the weekend. I'd been looking forward to that for weeks, but now the only news I can give her is that I'm an unemployed loser. The worst part of all is that I bought an engagement ring for her. I decided to pop the question this weekend.

Now, I don't know if I should. Jamie deserves better than a screwed-up guy who doesn't even have a job. My secondary present for her isn't really a gift at all. Just something I thought might be useful.

None of that matters anymore. My life just got flushed down an industrial toilet.

Chapter Sixteen

Jamie

A sigh of pleasure whispers out of me as I walk into the Loch Fairbairn café at precisely ten o'clock, just as Gavin had asked me to do. We have never needed a timetable for our dates, but lately, he has seemed uneasy and a wee bit uncertain too. About what? Us? Me? My family? I know my brothers can be intimidating, but not to Gavin. He's a strong, braw man who would never run away from a fight.

Not that my brothers have ever tried to literally chase him away.

Just inside the café doors, I halt. Does my hair look all right? Maybe I should get out my comb and run it through my hair one last time. I have a feeling this might be the day when Gavin pops the big question. Dinnae know why I feel that way. My heart believes it, though. I glance down at my flower-print skirt and peasant blouse. It looks fine. I look fine. *No more dawdling, you silly lass.*

I march across the café with my skirt swishing and my head held high as I wend my way around the tables and chairs to reach Gavin. I grin at him.

He jumps up to pull a chair out for me. Though he smiles, it's rather subdued and seems almost anxious. He can't worry I'll say no to his proposal, can he?

Once we're both seated, he clasps his hands on the tabletop—and begins to wring them.

"Are you all right, Gav?"

"Uh, yeah, sure." He moves his hands to his lap. "You look really pretty today."

"Thank you."

He chose a table in the outdoor section of the café, beneath a striped awning, as if he wants as much privacy as possible. But now he fidgets and keeps glancing about like he's worried a boulder might crash down on his head from the clear blue sky.

I scoot my chair closer to his. "You dinnae seem all right. What's fashing you?"

"Nothing, I swear." He grasps the seat of my chair to pull it closer to him. Our faces are now within kissing distance, and his expression has become relaxed. But the way he licks his lips, coupled with his darkening irises, tells me he wants to snog. "Mind if I kiss you for an hour or two?"

"As long as you want, *mo chridhe*."

Gavin presses his mouth to mine, molding our lips to each other in the most languid and sensual manner, until I'm melting for him. When he slips his tongue between my lips, I sag into him. A soft wee moan whispers out of me. *Bod an Donais*, I love kissing this man. He tastes like coffee with two creams and three sugars, which is odd since I know he takes his coffee black with one sugar. Why did he change his preference?

That's the way I like my coffee, though.

With his mouth still touching mine, he gazes straight into my eyes. "Did you notice the coffee flavor? I know you don't like it when I kiss you after I've drunk black coffee."

"You did that for me? Och, Gav, you are the sweetest man."

"Anything for you, baby."

We go back to kissing, oblivious of anything that might be occurring around us. Nothing matters except the two of us inside this wee bubble of romance. We go on reveling in the kiss for so long that I lose track of time. This feels wonderful, especially since we haven't made love in three months. He always has an excuse for that, and it's usually work stress. But here, while we're enjoying each other's lips, none of that matters anymore.

At last, Gavin slowly pulls away, though his eyes remain closed. He exhales a long sigh before finally opening his eyes.

I glance round the café without moving my head, expecting to see other customers glaring at us and our flagrantly romantic display. But no one has paid any mind to us. We might as well have become invisible. Beyond our wee bubble of solitude, the sun shines and showers its warmth on us. Inside the café, Halloween decorations hang from the ceiling and from the awning, and still more decorate the tables and even the counter just inside the doorway.

Gavin finally pulls away, though only slightly.

I smile with my lips closed, which probably makes my cheeks dimple. "You must have something important to say, otherwise you'd never stop kissing me after only a few minutes."

Gavin loves to kiss me for so long that I lose track of time, and I love it when he does that. But now, he gazes at me steadily, as if he's considering how to start saying whatever it is he clearly wants to tell me. Abruptly, his expression turns anxious, and he swallows hard enough that I can see the movement in his throat. He winces the tiniest bit.

My smile falters. "What's wrong, Gav?"

"Nothing, I—Uh, well, see…"

"You can tell me, whatever it is." I peck a light kiss on his lips. "Do you trust me?"

He gulps again and stops blinking. "You know I do."

"Then tell me. I'm tougher than I look."

He just stares at me.

Is proposing such a difficult thing to do? I wouldn't think so, but then, I am not a man. They can be such numpties about love sometimes. "You think about it while I powder my nose."

"Your nose looks fine to me."

I laugh softly, charmed by his statement because it's such an innocently barmy thing to say. "It's a polite way of telling you I need to piss."

His brows shoot up, though I can't imagine that he's shocked that I used a vulgar word. Gavin hears me curse all the time.

I rise from my chair and kiss his forehead. "I'll be a minute."

After a brief trip to the restroom, I swiftly make my way through the café. I feel lighter today, as if I might float up into the sky. This has been the best day I've had in a long time, and I just know Gavin has something up his sleeve. But when I walk into the outdoor patio, I see him sitting at our table with his head bowed and his hands tightly clasped on the tabletop. Then he rubs his eyes.

Maybe he's just a wee bit anxious about popping the question.

"Here I am," I announce as I reclaim my seat beside Gavin. "What was it you wanted to talk about?"

He sits up straighter and lifts his chin.

"You okay?" I ask, tipping my head to study him. "The flight from America has you knackered, doesn't it? We can talk later."

"No," he snaps. "Now. We should, uh, talk now. I'm going home tomorrow."

I know that already. Why did he feel the need to remind me? Nerves, I assume. So, I lean toward him. "Go on, Gavin. I'm listening."

He winces again. Then he surreptitiously shoves a hand into his trouser pocket. Well, not that surreptitiously since I saw him do it. He clearly hoped I wouldn't notice.

Go on, Gavin, just do it. Ask me. He must know I'll say yes. How could he believe otherwise?

He yanks an object out of his pocket and…thrusts a slender, flat rectangular object at me. "This is for you. It's so you can get miles to use for travel expenses."

Miles? What the bloody sodding hell is he havering about? I gawp at the credit card he just offered me, unable to move or speak for several seconds that feel like hours. I gingerly accept the credit card, holding the very edge of one corner between my thumb and forefinger. I cannae help curling my lip, though not from disgust. It's from utter confusion. "I don't need miles, Gavin. We both fly on Rory's jet."

His face blanches. His eyes nearly bulge out of their sockets. His lips work as if he cannae cobble together even one sentence. And he clamps his fingers around the ring box. "I got one of those credit cards where you earn miles with every purchase. Made you an authorized user on it. This'll, uh, help pay for—expenses. When you visit me."

"You said this already." My lips begin to quiver. My pulse races, though not in a good way, and I feel the first sting of tears in my eyes. "I reminded you I don't need a bloody credit card. Is this why you brought me here? To a romantic restaurant? This is the important thing you needed to tell me? After eighteen months together, this is all you think I'm worth."

He shakes his head slowly, minutely, while his eyes remain wide. He says nothing.

Tears trickle down my cheeks even while I want to grab him by the throat and bash his head onto the table repeatedly. I love him, and he claims to love me. If that's true, how could he hand me a credit card as if it's a wonderful gift? He must have realized I'd assume he meant to ask me to marry him. After all these months, nearly two years together, this is what he thinks of me? I need a fucking credit card? No, I need *him*. I want to spend the rest of my life with Gavin Douglas. Yet he just smacked me in the face, metaphorically.

"You're an eejit, Gavin. A *bod ceann* and an eejit, and I'm done."

"Jamie—"

I leap out of my chair so quickly that it topples over, but I can't worry about that or anything right now. I fling the credit card at him. It lands on his lap. "I cannae do this anymore, Gavin. It's over."

"What?"

"I'm breaking up with you." I enunciate each word with knife-like precision, even while my throat tightens and tears pour down my cheeks. "Goodbye, forever."

While Gavin just sits there gawping at me, I rush out of the café and down the sidewalk, swerving down the side street where I'd parked my car. As I collapse onto the driver's seat and shut the door, I can no longer hold back my anguish. I cover my face with my hands and sob. But I only do that for a moment, then I realize that crying willnae help at all. So, I wipe away my tears and blow my nose.

In the rearview mirror, I can see my own face. My eyes are red, and my face is blotchy. *Mhac na galla*. This isn't the way I behave. I'm always cheerful and optimistic, but Gavin Douglas has taken all of that away from me. I still love him. I always will. But I dinnae know if we can ever repair the damage he caused simply by offering me a sodding credit card.

No, I will not let Gavin ruin my day or my outlook on life.

After a few moments of rest, I study myself in the mirror again. No more bloodshot eyes. No more blotchy face. I look like myself again.

But I still have a dilemma. Where should I go? Home? That means Aidan and Calli's house. I'd moved back in with them recently. Ugh, no, I can't run there. I might look better now, but I still feel like rubbish. Maybe a wee walk might refresh me. I climb out of my car and return to the corner where the café is. Gavin's car is gone, so at least I won't need to worry about bumping into him.

I am alone.

That solitary thought spurs the tears to gather once again in my eyes. *Bloody hell*. Look what Gavin has done to me. I march off down the street, away from the café, while I sniffle and wipe tears away from my eyes. Rory's office is two blocks away. I'll go there. Maybe my taciturn brother will offer to hunt down Gavin and batter him senseless. No, I dinnae want that. Because the worst part of all is that I will always love him, even if we never reconcile.

Gavin Douglas is the love of my life, that ersehole. How could he do this to me?

As I march down the pavement toward Rory's office, I experience something I have never felt before. I think it's what people call an epiphany. Usually, those are a good thing, aren't they? Mine is bloody awful. I've just realized that my relationship with Gavin must have been doomed from the start. His emotional damage has stood between us like a concrete wall ever since the day we met. He can't adjust to living in Scotland. He's made that clear, though he never specifically said so. My brothers might have found their true loves, but I am not that lucky.

Unless…

As I push through the door to Rory's outer office, I realize that I'm still conflicted about Gavin and always will be unless something changes. The only way this will end without both our hearts getting shattered is if he makes the next move.

Please, Gavin, fight for me.

How did Gavin win back Jamie?
Experience the rest of their story in
Gift-Wrapped in a Kilt **(Hot Scots, Book Four).**

Anna Durand is a bestselling, multi-award-winning author of contemporary and paranormal romance. Her books have earned bestseller status on every major retailer and wonderful reviews from readers around the world. But that's the boring spiel. Here are the really cool things you want to know about Anna!

Born on Lackland Air Force Base in Texas, Anna grew up moving here, there, and everywhere thanks to her dad's job as an instructor pilot. She's lived in Texas (twice), Mississippi, California (twice), Michigan (twice), and Alaska—and now Ohio.

As for her writing, Anna has always made up stories in her head, but she didn't write them down until her teen years. Those first awful books went into the trash can a few years later, though she learned a lot from those stories. Eventually, she would pen her first romance novel, the paranormal romance *Willpower*, and she's never looked back since.

Want even more details about Anna? Get access to her extended bio when you subscribe to her newsletter and download the free bonus ebook, *Hot Scots Confidential*. You'll also get hot deleted scenes, character interviews, fun facts, and more! Plus you'll receive audio bonus audiobook content.

Visit AnnaDurand.com to sign up.